Bob Moats

I0567328

Big Apple Murders

Copyright © 2014 by Bob Moats.

Rev. 0331141345

1

Big Apple Murders

ISBN – 978-0-9960845-3-6

For information and address:
Magic 1 Productions
P.O. Box 524, Fraser MI 48026-0524
Website: http://murdernovels.com
Cover by Bob Moats

Bob Moats

Other Jim Richards series books by Bob Moats

(In Series Order)
Classmate Murders
Vegas Showgirl Murders
Dominatrix Murders
Mistress Murders
Bridezilla Murders
Magic Murders
Strip Club Murders
Made-for-TV Murders
Mystery Cruise Murders
Talk Show Murders
Sin City Murders
Black Widow Murders
Vegas Vigilante Murders
Area 51 Murders
Mortuary Murders
Hypnotic Murders
Sunshine State Murders
Blue Suede Murders
Honky Tonk Murders
Dark Carnival Murders
Lipstick Murders
Pasta Murders
Talent Show Murders
Shyster Murders
Campground Murders
Network Murders
Reunion Murders
Big Apple Murders
Kennel Murders
Trick or Treat Murders
Santa Murders

For a preview or to purchase a book, go to
http://murdernovels.com

What a few people are saying about Murder Novels by Bob Moats

Mr. Moats, I just got your novel "Classmate Murders" and have to let you know, I read it in one evening. That is the first book I have ever done that with. That was the most enjoyable book I have ever read. I just started reading e-books, and reading again, after getting my wife a Kindle. This book was my 12th, and the best. I just got Las Vegas Showgirls to (read) tomorrow evening. I look forward to reading many of your books in this series. I have been searching for an author and books that were fun, entertaining reads. Your books are just the ticket.

Regards, A new fan, Bill from South Carolina

****

Another very nice comment submitted through my website from Micki P.:

"I recently was given a kindle for my 60th birthday. The first book I downloaded was the Classmate Murders and have now read every one of the them. Today I started on the Fatal Rejection series. Thank you for the wonderful ride with Jim and Penny and all the rest of the troop. I have laughed and giggled thru the stories, my poor family gave me the strangest looks! Now I really want a little Yorkie!! Fatal Rejection so far is another great read! I will be looking out for more of Jim Richards and since you are my #1 Author, anything of yours I can find."

Extra special thanks to:

Special thanks to Val Brooks who edited this book and for her great suggestions.

Thanks to the beta readers Cindy Gross Valstad, Susan Houghton and Al Norris.

Thank you to all the people who purchased this book. I hope you enjoy it as much as I enjoyed writing it for my faithful readers.

The Jim Richards Family of Readers is listed in the back of the book.

Big Apple Murders by Bob Moats

Chapter 1

"So, what do you do for a living?" the woman asked as she removed her dress and sat on the edge of the bed to remove her nylons.

"Don't start an interview with me. You're a hooker, so hook. I'm paying you for a couple hours in bed — the works. That doesn't mean talking." The man stripped down to his boxer shorts and excused himself to go into the bathroom.

The woman dropped the rest of her undergarments, and naked, crawled under the covers of the king size bed. Her john had picked one of the nicer hotels in New York City. They even went up to the room together as husband and wife. He said she wasn't dressed like a tart, which is why the man had chosen her. They didn't draw suspicion.

Bob Moats

She was relaxing, waiting for him to come out of the bathroom. The door finally opened. He stood in the doorway silhouetted by the light behind him. The main room was dark save for one small lamp in the far corner. It wasn't enough to fully illuminate the man.

He slowly walked towards the bed, the glow of the lamp revealing what he wore – a mask. A Halloween mask of a skeletal face covered his whole head. The woman thought of the Grim Reaper, only the man had no hooded robe on. He was naked.

"Hey, I didn't sign up for a kinky trip, mister. What's with the mask?" she said, as he crawled over to her on the bed.

"You are going to make love with the devil tonight, bitch," he spoke from behind the mask.

She started to move out of the bed, but he grabbed her and pulled a noose he had previously attached to the bed post around her neck. He tightened it so the woman couldn't move away. She wanted to scream, but he tightened it more, cutting off any sound she could have made.

"I want to look into your eyes as the life goes out of you," he said as he hovered over her and waited for her to strangle to death.

Big Apple Murders

~~*~~

Penny was not happy with her hair that morning. She was trying to get ready to leave for her job as host of her talk show in Las Vegas, which was broadcast through a network to the country.

"This won't do!" she yelled as she tried to get a brush through her hair. I was standing just outside her bathroom door wondering what her problem was. "Damn hair," she said as she fought with the brush.

"Babe, your make-up and hair girls will fix it. Besides, you look cute with your Albert Einstein hair-do," I said, and had to duck when the hair brush came flying out of her bathroom.

"I hate bed-head!" she yelled, as I retreated from the bedroom with Willy, our toy Yorkie, following at my heels. Even he knew it was good to get out of her way.

I went to the kitchen to make my toast, and I even fixed Penny's oatmeal. She came flying out and said not to bother with her breakfast. She was going in early to have her groupies fix her rat's nest. She always referred to her make-up girls as her groupies because they were always around for her. She gave me a quick kiss, lifted Willy into his travel purse, and was out the door in record time.

I hoped she didn't rush to work in her car. The chances of a ticket or an accident worried me. But I knew she was careful, she valued her life.

I sat munching on my toast and watching the local news. I hated to watch the news, but this morning I felt like it. I don't know why. I finished the toast and the news and got dressed to go into the office. The office was nicer now, with the addition built onto the side of my building for Lynn and Buck to have their own work space. Plus, there was a lounge for us to relax away from the perils of crime.

Lynn's been happier since leaving the homicide squad of LVMPD. She fit in with us at my investigating firm and was much happier being away from the grit and grime of murder and crime in Las Vegas. She also had a baby girl to take care of when she wasn't working a case. Her husband, and my friend, Deacon, had stayed with the police and had recently passed the lieutenant's test for promotion. Now, he had to wait for a slot to open up.

I headed out to my Crown Vic and drove to my building to see what was going on. I parked and went in the back, setting off Lacey's cowbell on the door. I waved to the camera and went down the hallway to my office. I went in and sat at my desk and waited for Lacey, my office manager and crazy person, to come bombing in to tell me about any new cases that came in. She didn't arrive.

I waited, still no Lacey. I was getting worried and went out to the main lobby where I found Lacey sitting at her desk typing on the computer.

"Typing your resume for another job, I hope?" I asked.

"I'm answering an email for you. It's from a group in New York that wants you to come out to a book convention to speak on your success as a writer and private investigator. I'm filling in the background information on your career in crime fighting."

"And how do you know what to write?" I asked.

She lifted my latest book and said, "I'm just copying what you wrote in your bio from your book. It's nice when you have it all made out for me."

"So, why do you think I'll accept this invitation to go out to New York for a book convention?"

"Because you love the attention and if you don't, I'll shoot you."

"I guess that's two good reasons. Where is this email that invited me?"

She lifted a paper from her desk and handed it over to me. It was a copy of the email that came to the firm. It wasn't even personally sent to me, although it did acknowledge me as the recipient. I read it over and was thinking about what they said would be an all-expenses paid visit to New York City. That intrigued me. If Penny could get the time off from her show, I'd accept. But, it seems, Lacey had already did it for me.

"This says that it will be over the four day Labor Day weekend. Maybe Penny could take the time off," I said to no one in particular. I looked at Lacey and said, "Penny and I just got back from my reunion last month in Michigan. I don't know about jumping across the country again so soon."

"As I said, you need to go there. You need to get away from this office, you're beginning to bug me," Lacey said with a wry smile.

"How am I bugging you?"

"You're always moping around. Since Lynn has been helping Las Vegas police with their cases, you've been bored. You won't take a cheating spouse case…"

"I don't like those, I've had enough of them," I interrupted her.

"…And there haven't been any meaty cases to take. Earl and Trapper jump on the hard-core ones because they pay attention to who comes in. You're always in your office meditating." She tried not to laugh, just making a snorting sound.

"Fine, I'll go to New York, but you'll miss me."

"Not with a gun I won't," she said with another snort.

I gave up and went back to my office. I sat at my desk looking around the room. It was a lot bigger now that Lynn had moved into her new office. I liked my privacy, and could take a nap when I wanted to. Or as Lacey called it, meditating.

I picked up the desk phone after checking my watch to see if Penny's show had finished taping and called her. I waited for it to ring, when I heard a ringing from outside my door. It stopped and I heard Penny on my phone saying, "Are you in your office?"

"Yes, where are you?" I had a feeling she was outside my office on her phone.

She peeked around the door and smiled. Willy came bounding in and stood up against my leg. Penny hung up and came in the room.

"So, I hear we're going to New York," she said.

"I wish Lacey would stop filling you in on my news. I wanted to tell you myself."

"Okay, I didn't hear anything from Lacey. So, what's new?"

"We're going to New York."

*

Chapter 2

"Why? I'll pretend like Lacey didn't tell me," she said with a smirk.

"Thank you. I've been asked to talk at a book conference about my life as a famous author and crime fighter."

She snorted like Lacey and said, "This sounds like our ocean cruise. You know that had murders. Is this going to be like that?"

"I hope not. My curse has to end. It will be in New York, I can feel it."

"You better be right or I'll drop you off the Empire State Building." She snorted again.

"Stop that, you sound like Lacey. Everyone is picking on me today."

"Everyone? Have you seen Buck or Trapper yet?"

"No, but I know they'll pick on me, too."

Penny stood and said, "I'll call Gordy and tell him I need that weekend off. You need to ask Buck to come along to protect us. New York is a dangerous town."

"And you grew up around Detroit. You survived. If I ask Buck, it will be because he's a friend and he might like going back to New York again. We may even visit the Traviano family. I'd like to visit Gino and Frances again."

"I'd like to see them, too. When did Buck go to New York?"

"You were sick, it was back when we went out with Earl to find the missing stripper for Angelo's cousin."

"Ah, yes. I remember now. You were also shot in New York, remember that? Gino and Frances flew me out to sit at your deathbed."

"I lived didn't I?"

"I'm wondering. Now, I have to go call Gordy and go shopping for my New York wardrobe," she said and left my office. I wasn't even going to say anything about her buying clothes.

Willy was resting on my desk where I put him. I reached over to scratch his ears, he loved that.

Buck startled me by popping in my open door. "Hey Jimmy, what's up?"

"My blood pressure. I'm surrounded with people who want to drive me crazy. Would you be interested in going back to New York with Penny and me?"

Buck sat in my client chair and smiled, "Is this about the book convention?"

"Damn, has Lacey put my trip in the company newsletter? Yes, I'm being asked to speak."

"I remember when that creepy woman came in your tiny office in Michigan to ask you to go on the ocean cruise for that writer's convention," Buck said with a laugh.

"Yep, but this is going to be on dry land this time, and hopefully no creepy woman."

"You hope. I'd be glad to go with you two. I'll keep the weekend open. Are you going to charter another jet like the one we had to go to Michigan?"

I thought on that, I didn't want to have to go through the indignity of commercial airlines. The private jet was nice, and less stressful. "I'll have to think on it. I'll let you know."

"Well, I'll be waiting. Now, I have a small case to find out who is stealing from a convenience store over on Tropicana. They don't know if it's a customer or an employee."

"Don't they have one of your guards there?" I asked.

"There is, but the guards are only on duty at night. Most of the thefts are during the day." Buck stood and said, "Let me know more about New York. This time don't get shot." He laughed and went out of the room.

"Again, being picked on. Now, I need Trapper to bash me." I stood and picked up Willy. I went into the new addition to the building to see if Lynn was in.

16

"Hey, Jim. Are you checking on me?"

"You don't need checking. How's your new office doing? Getting settled in?"

"I love it. When I was with LVMPD, my office was like a way station for everyone. This is so quiet here, I could fall asleep."

"Never say sleep, say you are meditating. It works for me. Heard from Deacon about his promotion?"

"He's waiting for an opening. There are two Lieutenants who are scheduled to rotate out. One is in Vice and the other is in OCU."

"I think Deacon would like Vice over the Organized Crime Unit. He spent time in Vice before, so he knows the routine."

"True. I didn't like him in Vice, but I wasn't going to tell him. Too many hookers and trouble he could get into," she said with a smile.

"Not Deacon. He's like a duck, he mates for life and never strays."

"He's hardly a duck, more like a rhino," she said.

"I don't know if rhinos mate for life. Doesn't matter, he'd never cheat on you."

"He knows I'd shoot him if he did." Lynn's phone rang and she looked at it. The light was showing it was Lacey from up front. "Excuse me, Lacey is calling." She lifted the phone and answered.

I looked at Willy and said, "Lacey never calls me, she loves to bother me in person." Willy licked my hand.

"Thanks Lacey, I'll be right up." She hung up and said, "I'm being requested to talk to someone in the lobby. Care to follow?"

"Sure," I said and we left the office.

The halls in the new addition were nice. I could see the feminine touch from Penny, Lynn and Lacey — light blue paint and, of course, paintings. The same kind that Penny and my daughter Carol had bought for her apartment. We went through the door to the lobby and found a woman standing at the counter.

Lacey stood and said, "Lynn, this is Casey Weller. She needs to see you."

Lynn went to the woman and said, "I'm Lynn DeAngelo, may I help you?"

18

"A police detective named Greg Warren told me to see you. He said you could help. My husband is being accused of kidnapping a child. The police have no proof that he did this, but they are detaining him until they have more information. They are ready to turn him over to the FBI and I need someone to find out why he's being set-up."

Lynn looked to me and said, "I'll take Mrs. Weller to my office, care to join us?"

I agreed and we went to her office. Once everyone was seated, Lynn started. "Mrs.Weller, start from the beginning. Why do you think your husband is being set-up, and who is the kidnapped child?"

"Dale, my husband, had his phone stolen and it was the one used to make the ransom call for the child of a casino owner, Nathan Reid."

"Reid? He owns the Starburst Casino over by Boulder Highway." I said. "He has a son named Harry."

"Yes, Dale didn't report his phone stolen since the police won't bother to look for it. So, he has no proof that he didn't have the phone when the call was made."

"But, they don't have proof he was connected to the kidnapping?" Lynn asked.

"No, but it was his phone, which is why they are holding him."

"Who is the detective in charge of the kidnapping?" Lynn asked.

"For the police, it's a man named Morton. I don't know his first name." She was starting to tear up. I reached for a tissue from the box on Lynn's file cabinet next to her desk. I handed the tissue to the woman. "They have FBI agents coming in to take over the situation. I don't know who's in charge of that."

"What precinct is he at?" Lynn asked.

"He's at the one on Las Vegas Boulevard, by Russell. That's where they are holding him, but I heard they may move him to the one on Harmon."

"I can call to see what his status is, and then we can go from there. I'll need some information from you." Lynn handed the woman a pad and pencil. "Write down your contact number and address. Everything about your husband you can give me. What does your husband do?"

"He works at a gas station. We just barely survive on what he makes. This is really going to hurt us now that he's in jail. If he doesn't lose his job from all this."

While the woman was writing, Lynn excused herself and asked me to follow. We went out in the hall and Lynn turned to me.

"I feel sorry for this woman. I don't think the police have much on the husband, so far. I'll call and find out. My question is, do I charge this woman for services?" Lynn asked.

"My feeling is some cases deserve pro-bono service. I've worked many times without charging. With this case, I'd say we don't charge her."

"Good, it will be one less worry she'll have."

*

Chapter 3

"I hope he doesn't lose his job over this. Some companies can be nasty about arrests."

"If he does, I'll ask Buck to see if they can get him into the guards. Can't be any worse than working at a gas station," I said.

"I'll let her know, that may help her mood. Thanks, I can handle this now. I appreciate you sitting in."

"Hope it works out with the husband. I'll talk later," I said and went down to Buck's office. He wasn't in.

I went back over to my office and relaxed a while. I turned on the TV in my office and watched Penny's show, which had already started. It always felt strange to me to see her on TV, especially since she was out spending money on clothes at the same time.

About an hour later, after I meditated in my desk chair, Penny came back in. She had about four or five packages, they were bunched together. She dropped them on my couch and came to my desk, sitting in the client chair.

"Guess what?" she said.

"How many guesses do I get?"

"Only one, but I'll tell you. I called Gordy about us going to New York and he loved the idea. I guess there have been some inquiries from NBC wanting to have me as a guest on their morning show. He said he'd arrange for the time and date and let me know. Now we both have a reason to go to New York. Isn't that nice?"

"Splendid, but you're on a rival network. Does that make a difference?"

"Nope, they do want to talk to me about my show, but mostly about all the crimes we have been involved in."

"Sure, you can list all the times you were kidnapped or held hostage, or how you bashed the bad guys with a pipe or fire extinguisher? Oh, and don't forget your sharpshooting skills at winging them. I especially liked when you shot Nick North in the arm as he was going to shoot me. I appreciated that one."

"Don't be surprised if they want you to be on the show, too. You could promote your books and the book convention." Penny said with a smile.

"I'll think about it. What all did you buy to add to the tons of clothing you already have?" I knew as soon I said it, I shouldn't have. Now, I was going to have to watch as she pulled out every item to show me. That could take days.

She surprised me and just gave me a quick verbal rundown of what she bought. Then she stood and asked, "Is Lynn in?"

"She was in about an hour and a half ago, but she took a case, so I don't know if she's still in." I answered.

"I'll go see, be back in a bit." She left the room and Willy was now standing at the edge of the desk yipping at her. I put him down on the floor and he shot out of the room. "I see where your loyalties are, dog."

I looked over to the bundles of her new clothing and thought about doing some clothes shopping myself. I'm not a clothes horse, so my best suit was about four years old. I'd need to look good for all the book people, or possibly the morning show. Maybe I'd take a trip to the mall and see what I could find. But, I wouldn't tell Penny. She'd take it as an invitation, and we'd be in the store all day.

I stood and went out, approaching Lacey at her desk. "Did Lynn leave or is she still here?" I asked her.

"She's still in, with Penny now."

I thanked her and went to Lynn's office again. The two were sitting, talking about something. I wasn't nosy. They both looked at me.

"I have some errands to run, I'll see you back at the house later," I told Penny.

"Yeah, yeah, have fun. See ya later," she replied and I scooted out quickly before she asked what I was going to do. I could never lie outright to her, she always knew when I was. I'm a firm believer that it's not a lie if you just don't say anything. That's withholding facts, but not lying. Lying is when you actually say one thing, but you're saying something that's not true. Anyways, I just wasn't going to say where I was going.

Two hours and five hundred dollars later, I arrived at our home, finding Penny in the pool. I put my new clothing in my closet and then went out to watch her swim. Penny was resting with Willy on a lounger and smiled when I came up.

"What were you up to for so long?" she asked me.

"Did a little shopping for a new suit to wear to the convention. I also bought some new pants and shirts," I said and sat next to her.

"You should have told me, I could have gone with you."

I just looked at her. She smiled. "Yeah, I know, you aren't crazy about shopping with me."

"Crazy is the operative word. What were you and Lynn plotting?"

"I can't say right now. It's something I asked Lynn to do for me. Trust me and don't ask."

"Will you tell me eventually?" I asked.

"Yes, you'll know when it's time."

"My birthday isn't until next March, so it can't be a surprise party."

"I said to not ask, please. I'll tell you in time."

"Okay, but it'll bug me."

"Good, I like it when I bug you." She swung her great legs over the side of the lounger and stood. "Now, I'm going to get dressed and we can go to Angelo's for a nice dinner."

I didn't disagree with that.

~~*~~

Lynn entered the Harmon Avenue precinct to find Detective Saul Morton. The desk officer recognized her.

"Hey, Lynn. I hear you left the force?" he asked with a smile.

"Sure did, Charlie, and life is so much better now. I'm working private for Jim Richards' firm. Is Saul Morton in?"

"I'll check," he said and made a call. He hung up and said, "He's in his cubicle. Last on the right in the back. Just a heads up, they got FBI crawling around in there for the kidnapping case."

"Good to know, thanks." Lynn went through the security doors to where Morton had his desk. She could see a bunch of suits loitering around a door off the side of the room. She went to the box where Morton was sitting.

"Saul Morton?" Lynn asked.

He looked up from the file he was studying and smiled seeing her. "You're Lynn Carter, oh, sorry, Lynn DeAngelo, now."

"Thanks, I am. I need some info on your suspect, Dale Weller. I'm a P.I. now, and his wife hired me to help him. I don't want to step on any toes here, but could you help me?"

"No problem, he's still under suspicion, but they're not sure if he's involved. We're holding him until the Feebies check him out further."

"When did the Feds get here?"

"About an hour ago. They took over our conference room to set up their command center. The kidnapped kid was Nathan Reid's son and he's hot to get his son back. He's in the room with the Feds. Want to see Weller?"

"If I could, thanks."

"No problem, he's still my collar, whether the Feds like it or not. Follow me." He stood and took Lynn into the holding area and to a cell where one man sat. He looked up as they came to him.

"Any word as to when I can get out of here?" he asked excitedly as he stood.

"Take it easy, they'll get to you soon enough. This is former police Lieutenant Lynn DeAngelo, now a P.I. hired by your wife to help you."

Weller looked at Lynn and asked, "How's my wife, is she all right?"

"She's fine, Mr. Weller," she said to the man. "Where can we talk?" she asked Morton.

"I'd take him to interrogation, but I know the Feebies would bust a gut. Can you talk here?"

"I guess so. Don't want to anger the Feds," she said with a smirk.

"May I call you Dale?" she asked the man.

"Sure."

"You said you lost your phone, the one used to make the kidnapping call?"

"I did. Last time I had it was at my job. I set it on the counter while I helped a customer. I went to pick it up and it was gone. I explained this to Detective Morton."

Morton said, "I had no reason to disbelieve him, but we have to investigate."

Lynn said, "If you don't mind, I may do a little investigating on my own."

*

Chapter 4

"Investigate all you want. Less work I have to do, and maybe get the Feds off my back, too," Morton replied.

"Dale, where do you work?"

"At the Gas'N'Go on Flamingo, by Koval."

"When did you lose your phone, day and time?"

"I know exactly, it was last Wednesday, at three in the afternoon."

Lynn looked at Morton. "Did you check surveillance cameras at the station?"

"Ah...geez, no we didn't. When the call came in for the ransom, we found out the phone belonged to Weller. We just assumed he was in on it and his stolen phone story was bogus."

"How did you know the phone was Weller's?"

"Simple, caller ID. It came up on Reid's phone at his house when he got the first call."

"The kidnappers were trying to delay by you chasing down the wrong man. I'm going to check on who may have grabbed his phone. If the cameras were working, it may have recorded the theft."

"Mind if I go with you? I'd like to get away from all these suits. They make me nervous," he said with a big grin.

"It'd be a pleasure, and you can verify the theft of the phone if the camera caught it." Lynn looked back to Weller. "Do you know if your cameras work?"

"Yeah, they work good and they keep the tapes for a week."

"Good, then they should still have them." She turned to Morton, "Shall we go?"

Morton told another detective he was leaving and the two went to Lynn's car. They drove to the station and found the manager. They asked if they could see the tapes from the day in question.

"I can run those for you, if I can find them. Hold on, I'll see." The young man went into the back room followed by Lynn and Morton.

The manager pulled out a tape and put it in an extra machine on his desk. He ran the tape to the point Lynn told him to go to. "This is last Wednesday, as you can see by the read-out. You said around 3 pm?"

"That's what we were told," Lynn said.

He ran the machine ahead and slowed it around the three o' clock reading. They stood watching Weller taking care of customers. Then they could see Weller taking a call on his cell phone.

"He had it there," Morton said.

They watched as a customer came up and Weller went to get cigarettes for the man after putting his phone down on the counter. When Weller's back was turned, the customer reached out and grabbed the phone.

"Got him!" Morton said excitedly. "I'll need this tape for our investigation."

"Do you have other tapes that would show this customer going to his car?" Lynn asked.

"Sure, hold on." The man brought out another tape. "This one is from the pumps. That customer should be on here."

"I'll take both, they'll be returned to you after we finish our investigation." Morton said and took the tapes. They thanked the manager and went back to the car.

"Lynn, this should help the Feds track the kidnappers. This is great."

"Saul, you go ahead and take credit for this find. I just wanted to help Weller"

"Well, Lynn, thanks. That sure is nice of you."

They arrived back at the precinct and went in. Morton called to one of his officers and said to cut Weller loose. He was in the clear. Lynn said she'd wait for him. Morton took the tapes to the FBI command center. Lynn could tell Morton was a happy cop at the moment.

About a half hour later, Weller came out of the holding cell exit and over to Lynn. She had been watching all the Feds running around making new plans with the new evidence. Morton said they got a car plate number off the tape and they were going to the driver's home. Morton left with the Feds, and Lynn took Weller to her car.

"Thanks for helping me. I really appreciate it." Weller told Lynn.

"Just let me know if you have any problems with your boss about this. I'll take care of it. Now, we have to get you home. I phoned ahead, your wife is waiting for you."

~~*~~

Penny was sitting at the snack bar watching me make a call to arrange our stay in New York. I talked to the person in charge of arrangements for the convention speakers, she said they had everything prepared for our visit.

"All set to go. Has Gordy called about your appearance on that morning show?" I asked.

"Last time I talked to him, he said he'd let me know. It would have to be either Friday or Monday. The show doesn't run on the weekend."

"I hope it's on Friday so you can give me a mention for the book convention."

"I doubt that people seeing me will flock to the convention to see you," she said with a grin.

"I'm hurt. Of course people will want to see me," I said as my cell phone buzzed. Caller ID said it was Lynn. "Hey Lynn, did you get your case solved?" I put the phone on speaker so Penny could hear.

"Sure did, and the FBI got the boy back safely, too, thanks to my brilliant deductions," Lynn replied.

"Got lucky, eh?" I asked.

"Sure did," she laughed. "Seems the detective in charge neglected to follow up on a surveillance recording and that gave the Feds the info to find the kidnapper. I'm happy they found the kid, but my concern was getting Weller free. The whole thing took only one afternoon. I'm sure I beat your fastest case."

I had to think on that, "Yep, I think you have the new record. I'll see you get a bonus in your next paycheck."

"I'll hold you to that," she said with a laugh. "Is Penny nearby?"

Penny said, "I'm right here, listening."

"Jim, I need to talk to Penny off the speaker."

"Fine, so plot against me," I said and clicked off the speaker, handing the phone to Penny. She got up and went into the kitchen, leaving me alone with Willy. I looked at him and said, "You don't keep secrets from me do you?"

He shook and gave me a small yip, then jumped off the couch and ran into the kitchen with Penny. "Traitor," I yelled after him.

Five minutes later, Penny came back out and handed me my phone. "So, you're still not going to tell me what's happening?" I asked.

"I'm sworn to secrecy. So, don't ask."

Big Apple Murders

"Not my birthday, our anniversary is months away, not your birthday. I can't think of what you can be up to."

"Good, so don't worry. It will be nice. Now, stop asking."

I stood and said, "I'm going to meditate in my office. Don't interrupt me."

She was giggling as I went down the hall to my home office. I sat at my desk and opened up the computer file to my latest book, about the murder of the runway models. I typed, trying to remember what had happened. I was starting to worry a little about my memory leaving me. My short term memory was about useless. I would think of something and then, a couple minutes later, I couldn't remember what I thought about. I should go see someone about that. Who would I see, a doctor or a shrink? I hoped I wasn't getting Alzheimer's.

I worked on a chapter and then shut down the computer. It was starting to get late and I was wearing down. Writing a book can be just as draining as walking a mile. I stood and went to the bedroom, where Penny was relaxing with a book. She had every e-reader made, most of them given to her from advertisers on her show, but she preferred the paper books. She also had on her glasses. She didn't bother to remove them this time; she was over me seeing her with them on.

"One of my books, I hope?" I asked as I undressed.

"Nah, I don't care for the author." She smiled and kept reading.

"Just for that worn-out crack, I'm not having sex with you tonight."

"Is that all it takes to keep you off me?"

"Hey, you're usually on the top, you know my back is getting too bad to bounce around."

"You just make that excuse so you don't have to do all the work."

"Sex is work?"

"With you it is."

She gave me a big smile and continued reading.

*

Chapter 5

Buck was like a little kid the morning we went to the private business section of McCarron Airport in the new van I bought for the firm. We left on Thursday because Penny was going to be on the *Today Show* first thing Friday morning. Gordy had it all arranged and the people at the studio were anxiously looking forward to having Penny as their guest. It was mentioned that they might bring me out for a short chat about my involvement in the crimes we had investigated.

I hired a commuter jet to take us to New York. The convention people had booked reservations for us on a commercial airline, but Penny and I didn't want anything to do with that. Buck was always nervous about going through TSA security, I didn't know why. I guess he just didn't like being poked and probed by strangers. Neither did I.

The jet was nice and the crew was friendly. We were seated, strapped in and ready to fly. Willy was in his dog cage looking like he wanted to bust out, but he'd have to wait until we were in the air. Buck was cracking jokes with the flight attendant and they were having a good time.

Penny was seated next to me and took my hand. She wasn't really fond of flying, but she tolerated it. She always told me she wasn't afraid of flying, it was crashing that bothered her. It bothered me, too.

The jet was in the air after a short wait on the runway. I loved to watch the scenery going by then dropping down from out the window as the jet rose up. Sin City grew smaller as we flew on towards New York.

Willy was running around the passenger area, much to the delight of the flight attendant, Lisa. Buck was still entertaining her and then she went to get us some food. I had arranged for meals and a movie. This time I got the movie "Air Force One", with Harrison Ford and Gary Oldman. It seemed appropriate for flying.

"What hotel are we staying at, sweetie?" Penny asked.

"They set us up in the New Yorker Hotel. I went to the internet last night and copied off some information from the hotel's website." I took a paper out of my jacket pocket and opened it up. I read from the sheet.

"This is what I got, 'The New Yorker is conveniently located at 34th Street and Eighth Avenue in Manhattan, across from Madison Square

Garden. The Empire State Building and Macy's are just down the street. The hotel is one block from New York Penn Station, two blocks from the Jacob Javits Convention Center, eight blocks from Times Square, and only a 15-minute cab ride from Central Park.' How's that sound?"

"Nice. Close to the Empire State Building, where I can throw you off," she giggled.

I looked back to Buck behind us. "How's that sound to you?"

"I like. Maybe they'll have something good going on in Madison Square Garden."

"I don't know if they still have boxing matches, but I'm sure they must have some events. I'll check after we get there." I said.

"I'm sure we'll be busy for the time we're out there; you with your books and me with my interview."

"I plan on visiting the city a little. Buck, Earl, and I didn't do much sight-seeing when we were out there. So, I expect to see more of the city this time."

"Yes, sweetie," Penny said, and then snickered.

Bob Moats

Our flight went well and we landed in New York at Kennedy Airport. I had called ahead for a car service to take us to the hotel. I barely remember going through New York City last time I was here. With the search for the missing girl, my mind wasn't on the view. So, this time I paid attention.

"I have to call Gordy to find out where I go for the show tomorrow morning, and who to see," Penny said.

"I'm sure we will find the place. I think the studios are at Rockefeller Center." I said.

"You only know that from the TV show *30 Rock*. This may be at a different place."

"We'll see. Wow, look at all the cabs. It's like no one owns a car." I said.

"Not many people do own a car in the city. I knew a couple bikers who lived here. One of them told me most people don't own cars." Buck said. "Plus, parking rates for a car in the city can cost as much as a small house. I once read about a man who went into a bank in New York City to borrow $5,000 and put his Rolls-Royce up for collateral. The bank gave him the loan and they put his car in their holding lot. The man came back two months later and paid back the loan, plus $15.00 interest. The banker said they found out he was a billionaire and asked why he borrowed $5,000. The man said he had to leave the country and it was his way to park his car in the city for two months for only $15.00."

We all laughed as the car pulled up to the hotel. We went in, followed by our baggage on a cart, and registered. I paid for the extra night past the free nights the convention was paying. I also had called ahead to get Buck a room. We went up to our rooms to unpack our things, and then Penny called Gordy.

"Hey, Gordy. We're here in New York. The weather is beautiful and warm for the Labor Day weekend. Now, where do I go to get on this show?" Penny said as she sat on the couch.

She listened while she reached for her purse and took out her small pad of paper and a pen. She scribbled something, and then said she'd call after the show. She hung up and smiled at me.

"30 Rockefeller Center. Okay, you were right. I have to be there by 6 AM to get ready. I hope they have a famous guest on," she said.

I stood there amazed. "You have some of the most famous actors and celebrities on *your* show, and you hope they have some famous guest on this show? I can't imagine who else is left that's famous enough to be on this show with you."

"Never can tell. Maybe they'll have the First Lady on." Penny stood, picked up Willy, and kissed me.

It was just after three in the afternoon, and we were hungry. Buck said he was going to look up a friend in the city, he'd see us later. I led Penny to the street and noticed she was feeling the effect of the city and all the people walking along the sidewalks.

"This town moves fast," she said.

"Not like Vegas where people take time to soak in the sights."

"I want a Coney dog, no offense, Willy," she said to the dog.

I spotted a Coney Island food stand and we went to it. We ordered at the counter and took our food to a stand up table on the sidewalk.

I was looking around the area, wondering where everyone was going. I looked to my right and found a man standing there facing me. "May I help you?" I asked.

"Maybe I can help you, my friend. I have a nice selection of watches for sale, if you'd like to peruse my stock," he said quickly.

Big Apple Murders

I pulled my jacket sleeve back and showed him my Rolex. "I think not. I'm good, thanks."

"Well, I have some nice genuine Louis Vuitton handbags for the lady. If she'd like to take a look at my stock." He was starting to bug me.

"I don't think so, if you know what I mean," I said as I pulled back my jacket to show him my Glock in its holster.

He saw the gun and smiled, "Sorry Officer, I'll leave you two to your food." He turned quickly and skittered off.

Penny was trying not to laugh, but couldn't hold it. "Officer? He assumed, since you showed your gun, that you were a cop?"

"I guess in New York only cops, gangsters, and gangbangers carry guns on their hip. I assume he went with cop."

"Yeah, you don't look like a gangster or a gangbanger. You do look like an overweight detective."

"Thank you, my dear, I love you too. After we finish this horse meat, I need to go register with the book people. Crime waits for no one."

*

Chapter 6

I wolfed down the last of my Coney, and then we took a walk down the street to the Javits Convention Center. The building was huge and mostly glass on the outside. I'm sure a porn convention would love this building, they could feature exhibitionist in the many windows to draw a crowd.

The book convention people were setting up the rooms where they would hold the event. I inquired as to where Mrs. Ethel Nixon was and the man I asked pointed her out.

"Mr. and Mrs. Richards! How good to see you made it, I am so happy," she said with a flourish of her hands.

I whispered to Penny, "She's going to be another crazy person."

"Be nice," she replied.

We approached her and she grabbed my hand, pumping it. Then she took Penny's hand and shook her hard enough that Penny was bouncing. I tried not to laugh.

Big Apple Murders

"I was worried that you wouldn't come. I'm so happy to see you. I'm putting you up as our guest of honor. So, be ready for a big crowd in the theatre."

"What night do I talk?" I asked.

"Sunday, you're the last to speak. You have the whole evening."

"Well, thank you," I said, with my best fake smile.

"I don't know if you are aware of it, but your publisher has set up a booth for your books. It would be so nice if you could sit and autograph them over the weekend."

"No, my publisher didn't warn me. I'll have to have a talk with him. Thanks for telling me this."

"I'll get you all signed in and get badges for you so you can have access to all the functions." She went off and I turned to Penny.

"I'm not going to sit the entire weekend signing books. I want to explore New York. I'm going to have a short talk with my publisher," I said.

We stood watching all the booths being set up for the various publishers and many for self-published authors hawking their own books. Mrs.

Nixon came back with our plastic cards on lanyards and gushed.

"We are so fortunate to have you appear as our guest speaker. Is your lovely wife going to join you?"

I looked at my wife and smiled. "Are you going to join me?"

"I guess so, if I have too," she replied quietly.

"Well, tell her that," I said motioning to Mrs. Nixon.

Penny turned to Mrs. Nixon. "I guess so, if I have to." She gave the woman a big grin.

"Mrs. Richards, you must be so proud to be married to such a famous author and detective?"

Penny whispered to me, "She doesn't know who I am."

"Possibly the only person in America," I whispered back. Then said to Nixon, "Don't you watch TV?"

"Good Gawd, no. Television rots the brain," she replied.

Big Apple Murders

"My wife is Penny Wickens, host of her own television talk show. She's on a national network broadcast across the country."

"Well, isn't that nice. I used to watch Oprah, until she left the air. Such a shame, she had many a great author on her show."

"That's all right Jim, don't worry about it. It's kind of a relief to not be recognized." She looked back to Nixon and asked, "Where's the powder room?" Nixon pointed it out.

I whispered again, "You're going in to cry, right?"

"Never. But if you hear wailing and gnashing of teeth, just ignore me." She smiled and went off.

I was alone with Mrs. Nixon. I felt the need to visit the men's room. "Actually, that sounds good. Where is the men's room?"

"I'll take you there," she said and led the way. I was hoping she didn't come in to help me.

She left me at the door and I thanked her. I went in and stood in the middle of the room wondering how long she'd wait out there. I hoped she was needed elsewhere.

About ten minutes later, I went to the door and listened. No sound, so I opened it and went out. Thankfully, she was nowhere to be seen.

I went back to the entrance to find Penny talking to a small group of people. She looked happy, so I figured she found some fans. She saw me and waved. I went to her.

"Jim, some of the authors do watch TV when they aren't writing." She smiled and introduced me. "This is my husband, the famous Jim Richards."

The crowd around her suddenly turned to me. I was being asked questions by everyone. Penny grinned from outside the crowd and went to a counter containing pamphlets for sightseeing around the city.

I entertained everyone briefly, and then said I had to go. They thanked me and went off. I went to Penny, who now had a handful of pamphlets. "So much to do, so little time," she said.

"Well, I plan on seeing everything. So, be prepared." I was studying the pass around my neck, it had a nice picture of me. Taken from one of my websites, I presumed. I looked to Penny's, they had her picture also. The name on her pass said, "Mrs. Jim Richards."

Big Apple Murders

I didn't like it when people used the husband's name for women. They have names, use them. "I'm taking your card and having it corrected," I said.

"Don't worry about it. The weekend will be over before you know it, and I'm not here to speak. I'll be there for you as your wife."

"Well, I'm sending a terse note to someone for this indignity," I said with a grin.

I heard a voice that curled my toes, it was Mrs. Nixon.

"There you two are. I was asking around and it seems that you are as famous as your husband, Mrs. Richards," she bubbled.

Penny was going to correct her on the last name, but I said to forget it. She agreed.

"I saw your publisher in the auditorium if you'd like to talk with him," she said.

Open invitation to leave her. "Yes, I would. Can you point out where the auditorium is?"

She motioned to a set of doors opening into a larger room. I thanked her and took Penny's arm, pulling her with me.

"Slow down and ease up on my arm."

"Sorry, I just want to get away from her. And, track down my publisher."

We entered the room and walked around looking at all the booths. I finally found mine. It was on the end of one of the rows and was well decorated. Nice full size poster of me. I don't know where they got that picture, but anyone with Photoshop could create it.

I heard a voice behind me. It was Morty, my publisher, calling my name.

"I hope you don't expect me to sit here all weekend signing books," I said before he could speak.

"Hell no, Jimmy. Just a couple hours so we can get pictures for our publicity on your books," he replied.

"One hour. It doesn't take long to take a couple pictures."

"Okay, tomorrow morning then."

"Can't do, Penny is going to be on the *Today Show* in the morning. Remember my wife?"

"Damn, I'm sorry, Penny. How are you?"

Big Apple Murders

"I'm fine, Morty. Thanks."

"Okay, tomorrow afternoon?" Morty was begging now.

"I'll let you know. Penny and I are going to explore the city. When we get back I'll consider sitting."

"Okay, I'll yield. Let me know when."

"How are my sales doing? You don't send me reports anymore." I asked.

"We're busy, I'll shoot out a report this week. You're doing great. Another bestseller."

"Why don't I believe you?"

"Come on Jim, I'm on your side. The more you make the more I make."

"As long as I get my fair share. Don't do any creative financing, or I'll hunt you down."

Morty stood with his mouth open. "I believe you would. I'm an honest man, Jim. I'd never cheat you."

"I hope so. Now, I have to go explore the city with my wife. I'll see you tomorrow." We left him standing at the booth.

Chapter 7

We left the convention center and headed to the Empire State Building. May as well start big, I figured. It was still open when we got there, so we took the elevator to the top.

"Why don't you go around that way and we'll meet in the middle and pretend we're Tom Hanks and Meg Ryan from *Sleepless in Seattle*." I said as we came out of the elevator.

"Who are you going to be, Tom or Meg?"

"You know how to ruin a great moment. I loved that film and wanted to be up here to relive it."

"Okay, Sweetie. See you around the other side," she said and went off.

I walked from the elevator pretending to have a son looking for his backpack and came around to where Tom and Meg met for the first time. Unfortunately, Meg wasn't there, neither was Penny. I hoped she hadn't been kidnapped again. I kept going around the observation platform and found her talking to an elderly couple.

She saw me and called me over. "Jim, this is Mr. and Mrs. Bentley. They met up here forty-nine years ago and are still together. Isn't that sweet?"

"Wow, that is. You two are the original Tom and Meg," I said, they gave me a knowing smile. "Did you meet on Valentine's day?"

The man spoke and said, "Nope, we met here on this day, just before Labor Day. We were in town on vacation and we both were up here around this time of night. This is something we do every year, just to keep us young."

I thought back to when Penny and I met again after forty-six years. It was in her TV studio dressing room and we had a bit of sex. I wondered if the Bentley's had sex here on the platform after they met. I doubted it.

"So, do you live in the city?" I asked.

"Nope, we're both from Rochester, and we lived less than a mile from each other. Isn't that a hoot?" Mr. Bentley said.

"Yep, quite a hoot," I agreed. "Well, we'll leave you two to reminisce. My wife and I have some play acting to do."

The woman finally spoke. "It's so nice to meet you Ms. Wickens, I watch your show every day."

"Thanks, I'll say hi to you on my next show when I get back to Vegas," Penny said.

We left the couple and went around the front to where Tom and Meg first met. It was getting dark, the city was all lit up and looking beautiful. We stood there for a while soaking in the city, when a man came around and said they were closing the platform.

"Just like when Tom and Meg had to go back down. The movie ended there," I said.

"Did they live happily for forty-nine years like the Bentleys?"

"I guess so. They did a good number of movies together." We went back down on the elevator.

Leaving the building, Penny said she had enough of exploring and she had an early morning call for the show. Our hotel was just up the street so we walked towards it.

It was dark and no one else was on the street, just us and three men following behind us.

Penny said, "Where's Buck when he's needed." I could tell she was tense when she brought her purse around to the front. I heard a voice behind us.

"Yo, where you two going?"

I looked back and said, "To our hotel to have great sex."

Penny said quietly, "Don't encourage them."

I laughed and put my hand on my Glock.

"Yo, maybe we can help have sex with such a sexy woman?"

"I don't think so," I said.

"You don't think so! That's funny, old man. What makes you think we won't take her and have our way with her?"

I stopped and turned, "Aw, you shouldn't have called me an old man. That wasn't nice."

"Okay, old fucker. How's that?" the weasel said.

"Just for that I'm going to have to kill you," I said as I pulled my Glock. Penny was next to me and had her .38 Smith and Wesson out. The men all gave shocked looks and turned to run. As they were going down the street I yelled, "Bang."

Two of the men ducked and went in another direction. I had to laugh.

"They're brave when they don't have a gun in their face," I said.

"I'd feel better if we were back in our hotel."

"Almost there, babe."

We arrived back to the hotel. The street in front of the building was busy with cabs dropping off people. Penny and I went to our room and in to relax. I took out my cell phone and called Buck. He didn't answer, but I wasn't worried. He was with friends, or so he said. I'd call later.

Willy was bouncing around, mad at us for leaving him in the room. We wanted to be sure it was safe in the city before we took him out, and Willy doesn't carry a gun.

Penny was spreading our personal bed sheets that we brought with us after stripping the bed of the hotel sheets. Hotel sheets may be laundered, but never fully clean. I had seen too many forensic shows where the sheets had all sorts of body fluids in them. We brought our own to be sure they were clean.

Penny took a quick shower and dried off. I would have joined her, but she was quick. After I did my nightly thing in the bathroom I joined her in bed. She was already asleep.

So much for sex on our first night in New York.

I laid back and turned on the TV with the remote. I left the sound on low so as not to disturb her. I watched Jay Leno, thinking about how he was in the same studio that Penny was going to be in tomorrow. Neat.

I fell asleep without turning the TV off until I woke around four am. I turned it off and looked to my wife. She was so pretty in the light from the bathroom. I turned over and went back to sleep.

Morning came quickly, and Willy was licking my face. I wondered how we would feed him since we used up his food on the plane. I guess he'd have to eat human food from room service. I got up and called down to see what we could get. The man who answered said there was a menu in our room. I saw it and quickly read it. I said I'd call back.

"Do you want breakfast, babe?" I asked Penny.

"No, I'm nervous enough without having food in my stomach," she replied.

"I'm getting toast for me and something for Willy."

"Fine, just don't mention food until I'm done with the show."

"You got it." I called room service again and gave them my order. They said it would be up shortly.

I called Buck again, he answered after three rings. "Hey, Jim, how's everything?" he said with a smile I could hear through the phone.

"Did you have a nice visit with your friends?"

"I did. Had a good time. We talked all night. I just got in about an hour ago."

"You'll need some sleep."

"No, sir. I'm good. I want to go with you to the show to see how they do it. I've watched Penny's show enough."

"I'm sure it's the same. We'll be leaving in a half hour to get there for her make-up. Meet us at our room."

"I'll do that. See ya shortly." He hung up and so did I.

Big Apple Murders

"Is Buck still alive?" Penny asked as she came out of the bathroom looking beautiful.

"He had a busy night but wants to go with us. He'll meet us here in half an hour."

"Good, I want to get there in time to talk to anyone who knows what I'm supposed to do. I don't have my stage manager here with me."

Room service arrived with my toast and some food for Willy. We both gobbled it down before Penny could see us eat.

She finished getting ready. I put Willy in his travel purse and I went to answer a knocking on the door, it was Buck. We finished up in the room and went down to the lobby.

I asked for a cab from the doorman. He flagged one down and we got in. I gave the cabby the address and we were there in no time after bouncing around the back seat. He came to a quick stop at the front of the impressive building. We went in and I asked a person at the front desk where the *Today Show* was located. She gave us directions and we went that way. The building was a mass of confusion. Everyone running around getting ready for shows, I imagined.

We found the studio, and some woman came rushing up and pulled Penny to a room. Buck and I followed the best we could and found Penny in a chair getting make-up applied.

The woman said, "Are you Jim Richards?"

I said I was, and she said, "Come with me."

*

Chapter 8

Buck was trying to keep up with us while this woman led me to another room. Two women took me by the arms, sat me down, and proceeded to apply make-up to my face. I could see Buck at the door trying not to laugh.

"Shut up," I tried to tell him, but I was having a hard time talking with them wiping my face.

Once they finished, the first woman pulled me from the chair and took me down a long hall, Buck in pursuit. We came into a studio that was busy with people getting everything ready for the show. I recognized a few of the reporters, or commentators, or whatever they called themselves when they sat and gossiped about celebrities. Penny was standing off to the side being talked to by some man with wires all over his head. I presumed he was the stage manager.

Penny saw me and waved. The man looked over and then motioned to me to join them. Buck said he'd stay where he was. I went across the studio, being careful not to trip on the wires all over the floor.

"Jim Richards. So good to meet you." He took my hand and shook it. "I was explaining to your wife what she is going to do on today's show. If time permits, we may bring you on to add a little background to your adventures in Vegas. But don't feel bad if we run short of time. Excuse me," he said and went off.

"You look pretty, sweetie," she said to me. I just stared, wondering what brought that on. "Your make-up makes you look pretty."

"Ah, I see. It's new to me. I prefer handsome rather than pretty."

"Whatever. You look good. Maybe you can use this back in Vegas. You may get more attention."

"I'm not looking for attention. I like being anonymous, it's convenient. I can get away with things more easily if people don't notice me."

"I wouldn't worry about people noticing you. Most of the time you're invisible." She was called over to meet the hosts of the show before I could ask what she meant by her statement.

"I'm not invisible," I said to myself. "People notice me."

"Did you say something?" one of the crew near me asked.

"You can see me, right?"

"Uh, yeah. I can see you." He gave me a strange look and went off.

"See, not invisible," I said, feeling vindicated.

There was a flurry of activity and someone came over a P.A. saying they were ready to go to air.

I figured I'd just stand there and wait until called.

Everyone took their place and was ready to go. This studio wasn't much different than Penny's, except this one was much bigger. The manager called for a count-down and the show started. I had watched the show on TV a couple of times when I wanted to see a celebrity they may have had on, mostly the good looking women.

Big Apple Murders

The hosts were brought on and then they got into the show, introducing the guests. Penny was on with a couple other celebrities that had been on her show before. So she knew them well enough.

About forty minutes later, they introduced Penny and brought her out. She looked beautiful, as always. I loved watching her move. She sat and they talked about her show for a while, then got into the adventures in crime fighting.

"It's my husband's investigating firm that gets us into and out of trouble. We got back together, after forty-six years of separation, during the Classmate Murders, which they made into a fairly successful made-for-TV movie a couple years back. We've been investigating cases since then."

A woman host asked, "You moved from Michigan to Las Vegas where you got back into your network show. How's the city treating you?"

"Vegas is fabulous. It has everything you could need. Maybe I shouldn't build it up too much. Everyone will want to move there," she said with a laugh.

"I've been there, so I understand. Well, we thank you for joining our show all the way from Vegas. I'm sure you're anxious to get back"

"Well, my husband has to give a speech at the American Book Convention, so we have another couple days of sightseeing to do."

"Hope you enjoy your stay, we have to go to commercial and then we'll have Jody Reese on to talk about her new movie."

They cut away and Penny was whisked away from the small stage and a technician removed her wireless microphone. She came to where I was still standing, waiting for my big debut on the show.

"Sorry, sweetie. You missed your big opportunity to promote your speech."

"Yep, I'm still invisible. Shall we go get this goop off our faces?"

We went back to the make-up room and the women removed the goop. Buck was still chuckling as he watched me. We thanked the people from the show and went back out into the daylight.

"What shall we do now?" I asked Penny and Buck.

"Let's take a walk up Broadway, maybe see a show," Penny said.

"Works for me," Buck said.

Big Apple Murders

Penny mentioned *Motown, the Musical*.

"No way," I said. "Nothing to remind me of Detroit. Besides, Barry Gordy moved Motown to LA, so it no longer exists in Detroit except in memories. How about the *Book of Mormon*?"

"So you can get your chuckles knocking religion?" Penny asked.

"Fine then, we'll let Buck decide." I said. We turned to look at Buck as he stood looking around the area. He was like a deer caught in headlights. He suddenly came back from wherever he was and said, "How about *Mama Mia*? I'd like a good ABBA musical."

Penny smiled and said, "Buck, you're an old softy."

"Okay, I love ABBA, *Mama Mia* it is," I said and pulled my cell phone. I got on the Google app and found out where the musical was playing at, called to see if we could get tickets and reserved three seats. I love Android phones. About thirty minutes later we managed to get to Broadway and to the Winter Garden Theatre where our tickets were waiting.

The show was lively, fun and full of great ABBA tunes. We had a great time all the way through. It ended and we filed out to the bright daylight.

"I guess I should put in an appearance at my book booth. The fans will want my autograph," I said and Buck laughed. "What?" I asked him.

"You'll sign the books and then they'll end up on EBay," he replied.

"I don't care. As long as they buy the book from my publisher. Now we need a cab."

"I'll get it," Buck said and stepped out into the street, nearly being hit by a cab. It stopped just before him, as he said with a grin, "Here's one."

After my heart started again, we got in and told the cabby to go to the Javits Center. He roared off causing us to hang on for dear life. We arrived safely and got out as quickly as possible. He roared off after I paid him.

We went in the building and put on our passes. Buck didn't have one, so I had to register him at the door. I saw Mrs. Nixon and hid my face. Unfortunately, she saw Penny and came over.

"Mrs. Nixon, good to see you again," Penny said. I didn't agree, but kept it to myself.

Big Apple Murders

The woman was surprised by Buck, she was giving him the eye. "And who is this fine looking man?"

I figured that I could sick Nixon on Buck and she'd leave me alone. I just didn't care for the woman, my personal feelings. She was too overzealous and pompous.

"This is my associate, Buck Carson. He handles our tough cases and is our best bodyguard."

"Well, if I could hire him to guard me, I'd be happy," she said.

Nothing fazed Buck, "You can save your money, I'd be happy to guard you for free."

Nixon twittered and smiled. "Well, let's get you an all-access pass, so you can enjoy everything in the convention." She went to take care of signing in Buck. I was always amazed at how cool Buck could remain.

Nixon came back with a pass and a lanyard. She put it around Bucks neck, although he had to bend down. He grinned at us as she led him into the show. Poor bastard.

*

Chapter 9

Penny and I went into the show area to wander through all the book peddlers and authors hawking their wares. I saw a number of authors whom I admired for their books. I doubted they knew who I was by sight. Maybe after tomorrow's speech, I'd be a little more known.

We came around to the booth promoting my books. There was a good sized pile of them on the table and two young girls behind the table selling them. One of the girls asked me if I'd like to buy a book. I smiled and turned the book around to show my picture.

"That's Jim Richards, he wrote the book and will be here today autographing them," she said with innocence.

I smiled and held the book next to my face and said, "Look familiar?"

She grinned. "Wow, you look just like Mr. Richards!"

I put the book down and turned to Penny. "Invisible? Okay, you were right."

She was laughing and said, "Here comes Morty, he'll get this straightened out."

"Jimbo, glad you made it." Morty said, slapping me on the back. He turned to the girls and said, "This is Jim Richards, famous author of all these books."

I could see the girl looking shocked and turning red, I held out my hand to her. "Nice to meet you," I said.

"I'm sorry, Mr. Richards. I was just so excited to be here, I wasn't paying attention." She was trying not to stutter.

"First rule of investigating, pay attention to details." I turned to Morty and said, "Okay, I'm here. Do you have pens?"

"Shelly, pull that box out for Mr. Richards," he said to the girl. "Jim, sit and I'll go announce you." He turned and went off quickly.

"Announce me? How's he going to do that?" I wondered.

In response to my question, I heard Morty over the auditorium speakers. "Ladies and gentlemen, we have the famous writer and private investigator, Jim Richards, sitting in his book booth, aisle 5, last booth, signing his books. This is going to be a short visit as Mr. Richards has crimes to investigate, so rush over now." There was a loud click and the speakers went silent. Thankfully.

Penny was laughing behind me and came forward. The girl who didn't recognize me, Shelly, suddenly looked shocked. "Oh wow, you're Penny Wickens aren't you?"

"Fine, she recognizes you but not me." I said quietly to her.

"Yes, dear, I am. Pleasure to meet you." She held her hand out for the girl. "Mr. Richards is my husband."

"Wow, famous and married to a famous person. Double threat," she bubbled.

I went around the table of books and pulled a chair. People were starting to move up to the table. I looked to Shelly and the other girl and said, "Time to sell books."

Penny leaned over and kissed me, "I'm going to explore the show. I'll be back."

"Don't get kidnapped," I said and she stuck her tongue out as she walked away. I watched her, she moved so nicely from the rear.

Big Apple Murders

Morty came back to help sell books as people were moving in to get my autograph. I had traveled the country doing book signings a couple years back, but this was the first time I worked a big New York convention. I was a little overwhelmed by the number of people waiting now.

"Are you going to have enough books?" I asked Morty.

"Never fear, I got twenty more cases out back in a trailer. I came prepared."

"How are you keeping tabs on sales here? I want to get my proper share."

"I know how many books I brought, I subtract that number from what's left and that gives me the total sold."

I nodded as I signed a book for some elderly woman who was telling me all about my books she's read. I just sat nodding my head more.

After an hour, I was actually having fun, even though my hand was starting to cramp. I must have signed about five hundred books, by my rough estimate. I was watching Morty as I could tell he was delighted with the sales.

I had to take a bathroom break so called to Morty. "Need to take a break." I turned to the people waiting and said, "Folks, I have to go check the plumbing. I will return shortly."

Some people laughed and some groaned, but no one left the line. Now I was committed to return.

I stood and left the booth after asking Morty where the restrooms were. I headed that way wondering where Penny was off to. She probably found a group of fans and was sitting, holding court.

I found the restroom and went in, looking around the very clean room. I was almost bouncing as I approached the urinal, ready to do my business. I looked in the mirror just over from me above the washbasins. I could see a pair of shoes attached to legs in the only stall being used. I also noticed a hand hanging down next to the legs. It didn't look normal for someone sitting on a toilet. I finished my business and zipped up. I went to the sinks and called to the unknown man in the stall.

"Excuse me, I don't usually talk to people in toilet stalls, but are you alright?" I was loud enough for any person in the restroom to hear, but there was only me and the unknown man in the stall. "Are you alright?" I asked again. No reply.

I finished washing my hands and went to the stall, knocking on the door. "Hello? You okay in there?" Still no answer. Now, I was concerned.

Big Apple Murders

I tried to peek through the crack in the door and saw the man slumped over. He had a rope around his neck and he didn't look very much alive. The door wasn't lock and opened easily. I saw he was definitely dead, judging from past experience with bodies and the fact that his face was almost purple. I pulled my cell phone and dialed 911, explaining the situation.

I then dialed Morty and told him to come to the restroom, there was a problem. About two minutes later, Morty came busting in. "Jim, are you alright?"

"I'm fine, but he's not," I said, pointing into the stall. Morty turned about three shades of pale and turned away from the stall. I thought he might throw up, but he didn't.

The restroom door opened and two men came in. Morty yelled to get back out, this was a crime scene. The men looked mildly amused until they saw the man in the stall, then they left quickly.

"Do you know who he is?" I asked.

"Damned if I know. I don't know every person in the book world. Just my own people."

I moved carefully towards him trying not to disturb any evidence, I just wanted to see how he was tied. The rope was tied in a noose and was around his neck. I could see it was pulled tightly, enough to strangle him. I backed out of the stall and we waited for the police.

About twenty minutes later, there were three patrol officers in the room checking it out. After a few minutes the door opened and in walked a very big black man who I knew from my last trip to New York. Captain Lou Brege. He had been with the Organized Crime Unit while Buck, Earl and I hunted for our missing stripper from Michigan. I wondered why he was here, since this didn't seem like a mob hit. But then again, I wasn't aware of the murders of this nature, a rope around the neck.

"Captain Brege, good to see you again," I said.

He gave me a beady eye and then said, "I know you. I know who you are. Just don't remember your name. Wait! I know, Jim Richards. The private eye from Michigan with that cop, Earl Daws. How the hell did you get involved with this?"

I gave him a quick history of why I was there and how I moved to Vegas to open up a firm there. "Earl quit the Detroit police and is working at my firm now. If you remember my friend Buck, he's in the building somewhere." I almost forgot about Buck and wondered how he was doing with Mrs. Nixon.

I hoped he was not tied up somewhere, too.

Chapter 10

"A dead body!" Penny yelled in my face. "A murdered man!" She was yelling louder now. "I can't go anywhere with you and not have a body turn up." She was quieter now. "I don't believe it. That's it, we're through. I'm divorcing you on grounds of mental cruelty."

"Hey, I don't murder these people, I'm just around when they are murdered," I said as Brege was standing behind me listening.

I looked back and smiled at him. "It's not what you think. My wife thinks I have a curse that everywhere I go, someone is murdered. But it's not my fault."

Brege laughed loudly and said, "My wife feels the same way. But being a cop or a P.I., we have to expect this. Now, I need to hear what happened up to when you found the body?"

"Great, you even *found* the body this time," Penny mumbled behind me. I ignored her.

I explained what transpired from when I went to the restroom until now. "May I ask why you're here? Last I knew you were with OCU."

"I was, but I got pulled from there when I was a little rough on a mob figure. I nearly killed him. They took me out of Organized Crime and put me in Homicide. I guess they figured they wouldn't mind me killing a few murderers," he said with a big grin. "Did you know the vic?"

"I have no idea who he is. I'm sure you'll find out and tell me. I may have heard his name if he was an author."

Brege made a call on his cell phone and a few moments later one of the Forensic people came up to Brege and handed him a sealed plastic evidence bag. It contained a wallet. Brege looked at the ID through the plastic and said, "Arthur McWilliams. Ring a bell?" he asked me.

I thought on it and said, "No, doesn't sound familiar. You can ask my publisher, he may know," I said, pointing to Morty who was standing by the restroom door watching the flurry of activity. The ME had arrived and was bagging the body while the CSI team was going over the place.

"Hey, Morty!" I yelled to him. He turned, looking spooked, and then smiled when he realized it was me. I motioned to him to come over. He slowly came to us and asked what I needed him for.

"Morty, do you know an Arthur McWilliams?" I asked him.

He hesitated then said, "Uh, I think he's a writer over at Lipscott Publishing. Never met him, so I don't know him."

Brege was writing something down in a note pad, and then said, "I'll check with those people to see if he had anyone who wanted him dead."

"The noose seems a little strange, and in a public restroom. The killer had to be quick and strong to strangle the man before anyone saw him," I said. "I also noticed that the vic didn't have his pants down, so he probably wasn't in there to use the toilet."

"This could be related to a serial killer we've been hunting," Brege said. "We call him the Hangman because he uses a noose to kill. But so far, he's only murdered women, all prostitutes. Five to date that we know of. This breaks the pattern, so he's either changing that pattern or he had a problem with McWilliams. Maybe the vic knew him and threatened him with exposure."

Morty's cell phone buzzed and he excused himself. I was watching him as he went off to the side to answer the phone. He seemed agitated and was talking fast. I couldn't hear what he was saying as it was too noisy in the hallway of the convention center. People were gathering to see what was going on. I thought about the people who were waiting for my autograph. They probably got tired of waiting or found out that I was involved with a murder.

Penny poked me in the back and said, "I'm hungry. Can you tear yourself away from your murder to get something to eat?"

I looked to Brege and he smiled. "I don't think I'll need you for now. But you will have to make a formal statement for the record."

I handed him my card with my cell number. "Call anytime you need me." He agreed and I took Penny away from the scene. I noticed that Morty had disappeared. I wondered if he went back to the booth to apologize to people.

We found a food court and had gyros from one stand. It was nice they had set up the food court for all the busy people in the show. I was watching people go by and wondered how the murder took place. Maybe McWilliams was going to use the urinal and the killer came up behind him, throwing the noose over his neck and pulling him back to the stalls. Made sense to me. I should ask if McWilliams had his zipper open.

Big Apple Murders

"You're trying to solve the murder in your head, aren't you?" Penny said. "I should go over to all the romance author's booths to get away from you. I'm glad they have a wide variety of books here. Murder is not a way of life for anyone but you."

"I don't live for murder," I defended. "I also solve cheating spouses, robberies, embezzlements and other such boring cases. Murder just happens to fall into my firm."

"Yeah, well, with Lynn now working for you, she can take the murder cases. She's used to it."

"How come you don't say she's cursed with murders?"

"It's more fun with you. You get all flustered when we accuse you of your curse."

"So you admit I'm not cursed, you're just trying to fluster me."

"No, you are cursed," she said taking a bite of her food.

"I am not, stop saying that."

"See, you get flustered. It's cute."

I gave up and ate my food.

~~*~~

"You got the wrong man! I'm not paying you until you get the right man. And you weren't very subtle by leaving the dead body out in public!"

"Your photo of the guy sucks, I need a better photo. How am I supposed to take out your problem when I'm not really sure what he looks like? I should never have agreed to help you on this."

"You owe me! I helped you dispose of those women from your last bout of attacks. I'm not fond of mucking about in swamps to dump your kills. You need to do the dirty deeds yourself. I'm not happy helping you anyway. Now, finish the right man and I'm calling it quits."

"If I'm caught, you'll go down too. So, don't forget that. Now, shoot a good photo to my phone and where he will be."

"He's in the convention. I'll send a picture as soon as I can take one of him. And don't leave him lying about!" The man turned and left the small grove of trees on the side of the convention center, leaving the Hangman standing alone. He waited until the man was out of sight then turned back to the door he came out of.

Big Apple Murders

~~*~~

We had finished our meal and went back to the booth. The crowd of people had disbursed and only a few hanger-on's were left. I signed a couple more books before there was no one waiting. Penny had wandered off again, probably to find some good looking male romance writer to bother. I sat wondering where Morty was off to. He would never leave his cash alone with two bubble-headed teens. I was watching the crowd when I saw Morty come barreling down the aisle.

"Are you finished for the day?" he said breathlessly.

"You okay Morty? You look out of sorts."

"I'm fine, just all the excitement this afternoon. It gets to me and my asthma."

"I didn't know you had asthma?"

"Since I was a child. I have an inhaler which helps to relieve it," he said, then turned to the girls. "Now, how many books did we sell?"

Shelly picked up a sheet of paper and said, "647 books."

"Okay, not bad. Now Jim, I need you to move up to the table again, like you are signing a book. Girls, stand behind him holding the books."

"Why?" I asked.

Morty smiled and said, "Publicity. I need to get a picture of you."

*

Chapter 11

I smiled wide as Morty took a couple photos with his cell phone. I thought it odd that he used his phone. If he wanted good publicity photos, he should use a good digital camera. But that was Morty, he was cheap.

I looked over and saw Penny coming down the aisle with three women tailing her. She looked happy, so I figured they were groupies, and not her make-up women type of groupie.

She came up behind Morty and watched as he snapped off a couple more. I finally said, "Okay, Morty, that's enough."

He went through the photos on his phone and said they were good. "I'll see you later, I have to get one of these to the publicity department." He turned, nearly running into Penny. He excused himself and went around her.

"Very strange man," Penny said to herself, but I heard her and laughed. She came to me at the table. Shelly and her buddy were busy selling more books. I got up before I drew a crowd again and took Penny away from the table.

Penny said, "I called Frances and told her we were in New York. She asked us to come out to visit. It won't be the same without Angelo there."

"I called to ask him if he wanted to come with us, but he was busy, or so he said."

"Odd, a chance to visit his mom and he was busy."

"Angelo is a businessman now, not a leg breaker for the mob. He has responsibilities and I think his girlfriend is keeping him busy. He's a big boy, he'll come out when he's ready. When did you set us up to go?"

"Tonight. We're going for dinner."

"Well, it will be nice to have a home cooked meal, even if it is prepared by their cooks. We'll need a car."

"Frances is sending a limo to pick us up. I gave her the info to find us."

"You're just a little party planner aren't you?"

"A girl has to be prepared in these modern times. Now, we need to go back to our room and get dressed in our good clothes."

"I'm wearing good clothes. What's wrong with what I have on?"

"I have to dress you, your mother isn't here," she said with a snicker.

Morty was off somewhere, so I told Shelly that I was leaving. She smiled and said it was nice to meet me. Penny and I left the convention center and walked the couple of blocks to the hotel. It was daylight and the street was busy with people and cabs. A number of trucks filtered through the traffic carrying everything from clothing to food for restaurants, at least that's what the signage on the trucks said.

We got back to our room and I stopped. "Damn, I forgot about Buck." I pulled my cell phone and called him.

He came on after a couple rings and said, "Jim, rescue me," in a whisper.

I had visions of him being held captive by Mrs. Nixon and stifled a laugh. "Okay, we need you back at the hotel, we have to go visit Gino and Frances."

"Be there as soon as I lose this crazy woman," he said and hung up.

"Did you mention that Buck was with us when you talked to Frances?" I asked Penny.

"Yes, I did, and he's more than welcome to come with us."

"I feel bad now, sticking him with Nixon. I'll have to do something nice to make up for it," I said.

"Take him to a strip club, he'd like that."

"I don't know. I've seen enough strip clubs here to stay away from them. I nearly got shot in one by a crazy madam with a shot gun."

"Well, you'll think of something. Now, try on this suit," she said handing me the outfit.

I looked at it and thought of a funeral. "Does it have to be black?"

"Isn't that what all good mobsters wear?"

"I'm not a mobster, and that is right out of an old movie. Today they wear bright clothes to blend in. I don't know why I packed it."

"You didn't, I did. Your choices were tacky and I decided on a few clothes you would need."

"I bought this suit for a funeral four years ago."

"Oh yes, Marty Van Hought's funeral. It was a nice funeral."

"How can a funeral be nice? They are somber and respectful."

"Not the way you want to go. Are you still set on cremation?"

"I either burn here or in hell. What's the difference? You know I'm claustrophobic. I don't want to be in a coffin for all eternity."

"But you'll be dead, so you won't know you're in a coffin."

"Believe me, I'll know. Just scatter my ashes over the Vegas Valley desert. I'll be happy joining the sand. I'm not wearing black to Gino and Frances' home. I'll wear my blue suit. It is the one I'm wearing tomorrow night when I give my talk." I went into the bathroom to see if I needed a shave. I was good to go.

I heard Penny yell from the other room, "Do you know what you're going to say tomorrow night?"

"I worked on my speech before we came out here. I'll talk about my humble beginnings in crime fighting and then about my books."

"I was your humble beginnings. If you hadn't found out I had a school girl crush on you, I'm sure you would have gone off and got back into being a security guard."

I thought on that as I came out of the bathroom. "You know, if I hadn't developed a big crush for you and didn't know you had the hots for me back in high school, I may have gone back to my mundane life. I guess you saved me."

"I've saved you a number of times."

"Yes, and I haven't really thanked you enough. Do we have time for a quickie?"

"No, now get ready. Buck should be here any minute. I hope he has a suit." Penny went into the bathroom and closed the door. I went to the hallway door to look out and see if Buck was anywhere in sight. He startled me, as he was already standing at the door.

"Wow, you got here fast. Did you have to shoot Nixon?" I said.

"Nope, I told her you were involved with a crime and needed me. She was disappointed but I got away."

"Actually, I was involved with a crime. Murder. Some writer got strangled in the john. I found him and guess who's the cop in charge?"

"Lou Brege," Buck said, nonchalantly.

I just stared and then said, "How did you know?"

"I saw him in the lobby and he recognized me."

"You do stand out in a crowd. Did he tell you what happened?"

"He gave me a quick rundown. Your curse is at work."

"I don't have a curse!" I moaned.

"Yes, you do," Penny said, standing behind me. I gave her a dirty look and went back in the room. "Buck, do you have a suit you can wear to go to the Travianos?"

"I do. I'll go put it on and be back shortly," he said and went to his room. Penny came back to me as I was standing, thinking. "What's going on in your perverted little mind?"

"Nothing perverted. I was just realizing I've never seen Buck in a suit. A sport jacket, yes. But, never a suit. I'll need my camera."

"Just use your phone, it takes better pictures than your camera." She kissed me and went back to the bathroom.

Twenty minutes later, Buck returned looking very dapper in his suit. I took a couple quick pictures with my phone. I hoped the Travianos weren't wearing casual clothing or we'd look over dressed.

"So, how are we getting out there?" Buck asked.

"Frances said she'd send a limo to pick us up." I replied.

"Nifty, go in mob style. I hope it's not a hearse."

"I doubt that. Gino and his family don't go in for murder, I hope. They handle gambling and

90

numbers, that's all. Gino can't abide by drugs and prostitution. I guess that's one in his favor. It also keeps the Feds off of him. They're looking more towards the drug mobs and human trafficking."

"Uncle Sam doesn't like illegal gambling. They can't get their fair share of the ill-gotten gains," Buck said.

"True, but I think Gino's family is small potatoes, so they slide under the radar."

"Who's having potatoes?" Penny asked as she came out of the bathroom for the tenth time.

*

Chapter 12

We were ready for the car to pick us up at the front of the hotel. We stood on the edge of the sidewalk as the black Lincoln Town Car pulled up and out stepped Frances. Penny went to her and gave her a big hug.

"Penny, so good to see you again. Jim and Buck, welcome to New York, again." She grinned. "This time don't get shot, Jim."

"I don't plan on it. Not something I recommend to anyone," I replied.

"Shall we go back to the house," she said and we entered the car. The driver was holding the door for us and then got behind the wheel. We drove off through traffic towards the house on the north end of the city. It was more of a compound for the family. There must have been about twenty people living on the grounds. Between servants and the maintenance people who trimmed and kept the landscaping looking nice, it was a busy place. Then there were the made-men, who were part of Gino's small army, that protected the family and ran the business of illegal gambling.

"So, how is everyone back in Vegas?" Frances asked as she played with Willy on her lap. She enjoyed the pup and said she had a surprise for Willy when we got to her home.

"Angelo is really busy with his restaurant and his lady friend, Sophia. I'm wondering if he'll get married any time soon," I said. I knew she was wondering about him more than the others still back home.

"Sophia is a wonderful girl. She was so nice when I was out there last time. I wouldn't object if Angelo made her an honest woman," she said with a laugh. We made more small talk until we got to the huge gate that protected the driveway to the house. There were, of course, guards with very big guns at the gate and they waved us through.

I felt safe.

We exited the car and Gino came out to welcome us. He was looking much older than the last time I saw him. Of course I was in a hospital bed, hanging on for dear life. Gino and Frances were nice enough to even pay for my hospital stay and sent me the mini-limo for saving their future niece's life. I wouldn't recommend getting shot, but if it happens, it pays to have good friends. Even if they are a mob family.

"Gino, it's so good to see you looking healthy and alive," I said with a grin.

He leaned to me and said, "It's good to have big, armed men protecting your every move." He laughed and slapped me on the back. For a man a lot older than I, he was strong. I guess it was the good Italian genes.

"Penny, you are looking as sexy as ever," Gino said to my wife and gave her a big hug. "My wife should be jealous, so you'll have to excuse an old man if I give you too much attention while you are here."

"I'm not worried, he can't do much more than flirt with you," Frances said with a laugh.

"Whatever, let's go in and relax. Buck, so good you could come too. My home is yours, also. Come, my friends, let's go enjoy the day." The patriarch of the Traviano family led us inside. When we were in the vestibule, Gino said to follow him. He led us out the back of the house and into the backyard. There were tables set up and a huge barbecue flaming high. The cooks were all working over a huge piece of meat on the spit turning over the fire. It looked great. They had the table set up for a nice picnic and were bringing out bowls of covered foods.

Frances set Willy on the ground and called to one man standing at a door to the house. He smiled and opened the door and out popped a toy Yorkie just like Willy. But it had a big pink bow around its neck. Willy was bouncing around the pup and the two of them started running around the yard.

Penny was squealing with delight as they shot around her. "Frances! You got a dog like Willy."

"I did. I liked your puppy so much and needed the company, I went out and bought her. I call her Penelope."

Penny roared with laughter. She was even louder than after I tried to act sexy most nights. Penny said, "Frances, that is so cute. I hope we can tear Willy away when we leave."

"I'm sure he'll be alright. We'll let them play while we have our dinner," Frances said.

I leaned to Penny and whispered, "I think Frances wants to breed Penelope. Keep an eye on Willy."

"Like hell, Willy needs sex as much as you do. Leave him alone."

I had to admit it made sense. Go for it Willy, I mentally wished him well.

Gino called us all to the table and we did what he commanded. We sat and his people served us as if we were in a fancy restaurant. I guess it ran in the family, thinking of Angelo and his desire to have his own restaurant. Interesting, we were having a barbecue served up by servants.

We sat and had a great meal, complete with potato salad and every side dish we could imagine. I was watching Willy and Penelope run around the yard and occasionally disappear in the bushes. Lucky dog, going into the bushes for a little fun. I knew

Penny would never agree to that. She preferred a bed or a couch.

We finished our meal and Gino invited Buck and me to have a cigar in the library. I didn't care for cigars, but I also didn't want to offend Gino. We were walking to the library when my cell phone buzzed. I excused myself and went off the side.

"Hello," I answered. The caller ID had a New York area code, but no name. It was Detective Brege.

"Jim, the man murdered in the john was a writer for Lipscott Publishing, just like your publisher said. He wasn't familiar to you?"

"No, I didn't know him. I don't even know anyone at Lipscott Publishing, so he wasn't someone I was familiar with. Anything new on his murder?"

"Just the similarities to our Hangman. Same rope and same M.O. but this was different. Not a woman or hooker this time, and it was quick, like an afterthought. We don't have much to go on. I don't understand all these strange writers and publishers. This is a different world to me, so if you could give me a little help, I'd appreciate it."

He sounded a little baffled and I said, "I'd be happy to help."

"Do you want to ask your wife first?" he said with a laugh.

"I should, but she usually goes along with me. I'll talk to you tomorrow." I said and hung up.

"What do I usually go along with you on," came a voice from behind me. Penny had snuck up and listened to the end of my conversation.

I spun around and said, "Will you stop sneaking up behind me. I'd like to have a phone conversation without explaining it to you."

"Fine, but I'll get it out of you before the end of the night," she said, smiled and went off to the outside again.

I could have just told her, but her listening to my conversations had to stop. Yeah, right.

I went into the library where Buck and Gino were relaxing and smoking cigars. Gino smiled and pointed to an easy chair. There was a cigar on the seat and I picked it up. Gino leaned over and handed me a lighter. I had seen how they do this in the movies and on TV, so I lit up.

"Jim, how's Angelo doing with his restaurant?" Gino asked me.

"Fantastic. He has it running like clockwork. He loves the place and he's going to be famous in Vegas for it," I replied.

"I'm glad to hear that. Frances worries so much about her boy. I worry about Frances. If she's happy, I'm happy."

"Well, you have nothing to worry about with Angelo. He has everything in hand."

"Good, you keep an eye on him. I know you helped him financially to open the restaurant. Has he paid you back?"

"Long ago. The restaurant is doing well financially. Angelo still let me keep a small piece of the business, so I keep tabs on it."

"Good, you are a good man, Jim." He blew a big smoke ring and put his fist through it.

It reminded me of a target and he shot through the center. I was glad it was just smoke.

*

Chapter 13

We were enjoying the cigars. Well, I was trying to enjoy the cigar. I didn't want to offend Gino by refusing to smoke the foul thing. He got up and poured us brandy although I would have preferred a cold frosty mug of beer. Gino had money and stature, I would think his servants could roust out a cold mug of beer. Again I didn't want to offend Gino, but the brandy was good.

Gino sat and turned to Buck. "I hear you are now licensed as a private investigator?"

"Yes, I am. I've already gone out on a few cases by myself," Buck replied.

"Good. You've been with Jim a long time now."

"I have, and he helped me start my guard service. But that was not as stimulating as investigating. So, I'm happy now."

"Always good to be stimulated in your work." Gino took a sip of his brandy and smiled.

Big Apple Murders

Penny and Frances came into the library and stood quietly. Gino smiled and said, "What's on your mind, my dear?"

Frances came over and said, "I think these young folks have some exploring to do in New York before they go home Monday. We don't want to take up all their time."

"You are right my dear." He stood and said, "I've enjoyed seeing you all again. Now I have to go do my business. Have to keep the wheels turning on my empire." He laughed. "Good of you to join us. The driver will take you anywhere you want to go in the city. The car is at your disposal until you leave."

Buck and I stood and shook Gino's hand. We all went out to the front drive where the Lincoln Towne Car was waiting with the driver. We said our good-byes and got in. The driver asked from the front seat where we wanted to go.

I looked at Penny and she said to me, "Shall we go see if we can buy the Brooklyn Bridge?"

"I think it's been sold already. Let's go see the Statue of Liberty."

"I like that," she said and turned to the driver, "Statue of Liberty, please."

"Yes, ma'am," he said and drove off.

We spent a couple hours exploring the city. Our driver's name was Max and he took us to places that weren't on the tourist brochures. He was very friendly and had worked for Gino for over twenty years. Max was in his seventies, but didn't look a day over sixty. I felt young around him.

I asked if he could drop us off at the Javitz Center. I wanted to check out the show since the last time I was there I was tied up autographing books and being in the middle of a murder. So, I never saw much of the convention center itself.

"You better not find another body," Penny warned me.

"Not something I want either, babe," I said, and then turned to Buck. "Do you have someplace you want to see?"

"No, I'll go with you guys, as long as the crazy lady doesn't find me."

"I'll tell her you're body guarding Penny. That I hired you to keep her safe since there was a murderer roaming about."

"That works for me," he said, giving us his famous walrus grin.

Big Apple Murders

We entered the center showing our passes and went into the arena where everyone was hawking their books. We walked up and down the aisles checking out the new crop of books. I thought about the thousands of books being published or authors self-publishing their books. I was always afraid that my books would be buried by the mass of tomes fighting to be read. Luckily, my publisher was fairly smart when it came to promoting. It took a while, but all of my books were top sellers. Morty wanted me to do more functions, to get out in public, but I wasn't comfortable with being in crowds.

I saw Morty at my booth talking to people. Probably readers, but he was very animated in his spiel. I didn't want to go over to him, he'd put me to work. We passed by the booth quickly before he saw us.

Buck went up to get an autograph from a well-known porn star that had a book out about her life. I don't think Buck was so much interested in her book as just being close.

Penny and I were watching Buck talking up the star, when I felt someone hovering behind me. I turned and it was Brege. Penny looked back and groaned.

"You better not be here to say you found another body," Penny told the big detective.

"No, Ms. Wickens, I'm not. I'm here to talk to the publisher of our murdered man. May I borrow your husband? I've never been exposed to authors and publishers before and he can translate for me." He had such a disarming smile that Penny agreed.

"But only for a little while. Jim has to take Buck and me out for some night-life. You have any recommendations for safe fun?"

"Sure, in Las Vegas." He tried to suppress a smile. "There are a few nice places here in the city. I'll give Jim a list of those places. Just be sure to take Buck with you, he'd scare most trouble-makers."

I looked over to Buck, who was still chatting up the star. Then she wrote something on a pad, tore off the top sheet, and handed it to Buck. She leaned over the table and gave him a quick kiss then he turned to come back to us. I took him aside.

"Did you get her number, you wolf, you?"

"I did, she's going to be in Vegas next week and I got her cell phone number," he said with a twinkle in his eyes.

"What are you going to tell Maria? She may not appreciate your meeting up with a porn star," I said.

103

Buck was silent for a moment then said, "I was going to tell you about that. Maria and I have broken up. Don't tell Deacon, I want to do that. We both agreed it was better. She's more in love with her job than me and I hardly saw her enough. Besides, I think she was interested in one of the male dancers in the show."

"Well, better to end it now before you got married or something foolish like that."

"Agreed. Now where are we off to?"

"I need you to escort Penny around the show. I've been asked by Brege to help him interrogate a few people in the book world."

"No problem. I'll guard Penny with my life," he said and we went back to Penny and Brege. They were talking about the time I was looking for the missing stripper.

"Has he told you about all the strip clubs we went to?" I said.

"He didn't have to, you talk in your sleep and I interrogated you after you got back."

"Thank you my dear. I'll have to stay up nights now. Lou, are you ready to go?" I said to Brege.

He was suppressing a laugh again, and said. "I'm ready. Thanks, Penny, for the loan of your husband."

"As far as I'm concerned, you can keep him. Come on Buck, we have more exploring to do. Maybe I'll meet a nice author who will appreciate me." She took Buck's arm and pulled him away. He looked a little afraid. Penny was the only person who could do that to him. They went off as I watched them go.

I turned to Brege and said, "I'm yours now. Shall we go beat the truth out of a few publishers?"

We went off to the booth of Lipscott Publishing. There were three very attractive women manning the booth. Two men were standing at the back of the booth talking. Brege and I came up to the table as the women were trying to sell us a book. I took the book and saw it was written by our murdered vic.

I looked up to the girl and said, "Do you know about this author?"

"What do you mean? Is something wrong with him?" she replied.

I wondered if there was any word in the book world about the murder. I would have figured that Lipscott would be promoting the death to sell books.

Maybe they were respectable. I laughed at that thought.

"Who's in charge?" Brege said showing his badge.

The girl looked shocked, turned to the men behind her, and said, "Mr. Lipscott, the police want to talk to you."

*

Chapter 14

Both of the men looked to the girl, then to us. One man, who had bright gray hair and looked to be in his sixties, said something to the other younger man and then came to us. The younger man left the booth.

Brege held up his badge for the man. The man approached us and looked at it closer, then said, "How may I help you officers?"

"Well, I'm Detective Brege from homicide, this man is a civilian advisor. May we talk someplace more private?"

The man took us around the back of the booth. It was private, although we could still hear the convention noise filtering to us. But, it would work for an interrogation. Brege asked, "What's your name and position with Lipscott Publishing?"

"I'm Brandon Lipscott, I own the company. Well, me and a dozen investors own the company. I'm CEO and COO for the business. What can I do for you?"

"Do you know Arthur McWilliams?" Brege asked.

"Of course, he's our best author and best seller. What's wrong?"

"You haven't heard about the incident yesterday morning?"

"Incident, no. I just arrived in town about an hour ago. The young man I was talking to is my personal assistant. He picked me up from the airport and drove me here. I haven't even checked on sales yet. What's wrong with Art?"

"Well, Mr. Lipscott, I hate to break this to you but your best author is dead."

Lipscott looked like he was kicked in the balls by an angry woman. He staggered back and Brege caught him before he tripped over a stack of books. Brege helped the man to sit on a stack of boxes.

"How? When? Why?" Lipscott asked.

"That's what we are trying to determine. I was hoping you could tell us who may have had it in for McWilliams?"

"Oh man, every author out there who hoped to have his success. But really, there were no people who would murder him."

"I never said he was murdered."

"I just assumed since you asked who may have had it in for him. That sounds like murder to me."

"What type of books do you publish?" I asked.

"We handle cozy mysteries, police procedurals, action and suspense."

"No love and romance?"

Lipscott looked at me and made a face, "Heavens, no. We do well with murder novels. No, I don't know who would have wanted to kill Art. No one."

I asked, "Most authors have a dislike for other authors, did Art dislike anyone? Or feel threatened by anyone?"

"I recognize you, Mr. Richards. You write murder mysteries, maybe you hated Art?"

"I write true crime novels based on the cases through my investigating firm. I'd have no reason to kill McWilliams. I don't make up my stories, they happened."

Lipscott was silent, then said, "Honestly, Art was a great man. No one hated him or would want to kill him. This is so wrong."

"How was he set financially?" Brege asked.

"He had money. Not enough to murder him for. His book sales were doing well, but not huge money makers."

"Would his death cause his book sales to jump?" Brege asked.

"I hope you're not insinuating that I might have murdered him to gain financially? If he were a painter, his sales may increase. But an author is not a painter. His books are printed in the thousands, not like a single piece of artwork. No, my company wouldn't have gained much by his death."

Big Apple Murders

"Not accusing you or your company, just touching all bases." Brege said and looked at me. I didn't have anything more to ask that hadn't already been covered. I shrugged.

Lipscott was looking impatient. "How did he die? Robbery or drive-by shooting?"

"We're still investigating the reason for his death. All I can say is he was strangled here at the convention, in the john." Brege said. I noticed he didn't mention the rope or the suspicions about the Hangman.

"The john? Not a very noble place to die. I'll have our people put some kind of spin on it. If you don't need me any further, I have much to do now."

"No, go do your spinning. But if you hear anything, let me know." Brege handed the man his card.

"I'll call right away. Thank you for telling me this. I'd hate to hear it on the news before I was informed." He turned and led us out from behind the booth.

Brege and I stood in the aisle watching Lipscott talking to the sales girls. They looked shocked and then recovered. He was being animated in his speech. Probably rooting them on to sell more books because of his murder. The girls went back to the people at the booth and Lipscott took out his cell phone and called someone. Probably his P.R. people.

Brege said, "Would McWilliam's death be any gain for anyone?"

"Other than life insurance, I can't think of anything at the moment. If Lipscott had a huge insurance policy on McWilliams to cover his demise and future book sales, then that would be something to look at." I said.

"I'll get someone on their financials and see what he was worth dead to them. But how would Lipscott get hold of the Hangman to do the deed?"

"Maybe they set up the kill to look like the Hangman did it." I replied.

"But, that went off motive for the Hangman. He was only murdering prostitutes before. Murdering an affluent author is not his M.O., so I'd say the Hangman got paid well, or like you say, it was a copy-cat. If someone hired the Hangman, then they know his identity. The Hangman might go after them to cover himself."

Brege's cell phone buzzed and he answered. He listened for a moment and then asked where. He listened then hung up.

"Well, the Hangman is back on track. Dispatch sent out a call to a hotel, another hooker was murdered with a rope noose."

"Where did it happen?"

"Well, this is not going to make your wife very happy. It's at your hotel."

Crap, just what I didn't need. Now Penny will probably want to move to another hotel. "Any hotels that haven't had murders lately?" I asked smiling.

"Actually, the Hangman uses only the better hotels. You may have to take your wife to one of the run-down motels. I can mention a couple that haven't had a murder in over a year." Brege was enjoying my discomfort, I could tell.

"I'll try and see if I can get away without telling her." I said, and then jumped when I heard a voice from behind me.

"Get away without telling me what?" Penny asked.

Brege laughed and said, "You're on your own. I have to go to the crime scene." He turned and left me standing there trying to think of a way out of this.

"There was another murder, wasn't there? Was it here?" she asked while poking me in the ribs.

"No, it wasn't here. It was away from here. How did you and Buck enjoy the convention?"

"You're changing the subject. That worries me. Now tell me more about this new murder or you can sleep on the couch tonight."

I paused for effect, "It was in our hotel." I waited to be pounced on, but she just stood there. Now I was worried.

"Okay, so there was a murder in our hotel. Was it the same person who killed the book guy?"

"Looks that way. It was a hooker and she was strangled by a noose, just like the book guy."

"So it seems this killer is going after hookers and authors. I guess I don't have to worry." She also paused for effect. "But you do." She smiled and turned to Buck. "Buck, you'll have to sleep in our room tonight. I don't feel safe with Jim in the room. He can sleep in your room."

"It's doable. I'll move my bags when we get back." Buck was enjoying this.

"No one is moving anything. I can protect myself and you have your gun. So we'll be alright. Now, I'm hungry, let's go eat." I turned to lead them out. I could hear Penny talking to Buck behind me as we walked to the exit.

"He always gets hungry when he's nervous," she said.

"I've noticed that too," Buck said with a laugh.

I didn't turn, but said loudly, "You two can be replaced."

*

Chapter 15

We went out of the Javitz Center and walked down the street till we found a small restaurant in a row of buildings. We went in, lured by the great smell of steak grilling. I was in the right place. We sat ourselves at a table and waited for someone to come take our order.

"Are you done investigating with Detective Brege?" Penny asked me.

"I guess so. He has a new murder to check out. I was along to help with the publisher. Although I think Brege could have handled it himself. I think he likes me."

"Another fan? Or he just wants help with his case, like Deacon used to pull on you." Penny was grinning.

"Deacon appreciated my help. It was good when Lynn was away. Buck, what are you going to order?" I asked as Buck was studying the menu from the table.

"I'm fiercely hungry. I don't see a side of beef on here, so I'll start with the New York Strip Steak and work my way through the cow," he replied.

I really believed Buck could polish off a side of beef. Our female waiter came up and asked if we'd like something to drink. Buck ordered his usual Diet Sprite, Penny ordered a Pepsi and so did I.

The girl went off and Penny said, "I wonder if she's an aspiring Broadway actress?"

"Seems waiting tables is the way most of them start out," I said.

"So, why would someone murder a famous author, just so I know, in case you're murdered," Penny said to me with an evil grin.

Big Apple Murders

"My dear, I haven't any idea. Could be a rival author, but that's unlikely. A writer would murder him in a book, but not in real life. He may have had a gambling problem, but I doubt he would be killed for owing money. Now the murder was committed by the Hangman, or so it seems. He broke his motive of murdering hookers, so why this author?"

"Maybe he found out who the Hangman was," Buck said. "So he had to be silenced."

"Very true. He could have been researching for another book and made the discovery. The Hangman killed him to remain unknown. That's a good theory," I replied.

"Maybe the author moonlighted as a male prostitute and the Hangman was still in his element of murdering hookers," Penny said.

"I'm sure he had plenty of money, so a second job was out of the question."

"Maybe he did it as a way of getting into a new book. You know, studying the part," Penny said.

"I never have to play act my books because they actually happened. It makes it easy to write."

"I see a book brewing here in New York. The mysterious death of a writer by a well-known serial killer. I think you're going to stick your nose into this case," Penny said.

"Brege hasn't asked me to stick my nose into his case, so I'm not. But there may be a book in this. I'll, of course, keep tabs on what happens."

Our drinks came and we ordered our dinner. We talked about things we saw in the city earlier and I was wondering what happened to our driver. Maybe he went back to the Traviano compound. He had given me a card when he dropped us off at the convention center. I took it out and pulled out my cell phone. It rang a couple times then Max answered.

"Max, are you still nearby where you dropped us off?" I asked.

"No, Mr. Richards. I'm in front of the restaurant you're dining in," he replied.

I looked out the window of the restaurant and could see him parked across the street. I waved and he waved back.

"I didn't know you followed us?"

"Gino told me to stick with you. I followed you in the convention center and then out to the restaurant."

"I never saw you. You'd be a good P.I., being able to shadow people without being seen."

"Gino uses me to follow people he needs to keep an eye on. So I got good at it."

"Yes, you are. So, are you going to hang around all night?"

"Just until you don't need me anymore."

"All right, come on in, please, and at least let me feed you."

He hesitated then said, "I don't think Gino would want me doing that."

"Hey, I'm not going to say anything. Get in here, I don't want to be sitting here eating while you starve out there."

I could hear him laugh and he agreed. He came in and said he was going to sit at a table next to us, since there was no room at our small table. "Get whatever you want. Don't worry about cost. Just enjoy a good meal."

The girl came to him and took his order then went off. About ten minutes later our food came. We ate and it was very good.

I was satisfied with my steak, as was Buck. Or so he said. I was waiting for him to order another steak but, he said the one was plenty. I looked over to Max, he looked asleep.

"Max, how was your meal?"

His head snapped up and he said, "Delicious. Best in the city and I've eaten in all of them."

"Good, now we need to go back to the hotel. I'm sure the crime scene is secured." I said.

"I'll get the car and pull around. Thanks for the meal, Mr. Richards," Max said and stood. He went to the door and out. I watched him going across the street and to the car.

I gave the company credit card to the waitress and wrote in a generous tip on the bill. She smiled and went off.

"You're secretly hoping the crime scene is still being investigated, aren't you?" Penny asked.

Why tell her a story. "Yes, I'd like to know what is going on. It may have something to do with the author's murder."

"Well, we better step it up before they all go home," she said and stood. Buck followed her to the door as I gathered the credit card and receipt. Max had pulled the car around so it was on our side of the street. We got in and Max drove off.

We arrived at the hotel and I didn't see any police cars or coroner wagon. They may have parked in the back, so not to disturb the guests. I hoped they were still around.

We went in and I stopped one of the porters. "Are the police still at the scene of the crime?" I asked.

"I can't say, they're on the seventh floor, not my area. But I can check for you."

"No, that's all right, you told me what floor it was on so I'll just go up and see for myself. Thank you." I walked to Penny and Buck standing by the elevators.

"So are they still investigating?" Buck asked.

"Don't know, it wasn't his floor. But he did divulge the floor number so I can go see for myself."

"You're not going by yourself. I'm tired of not being in the thick of the evil deed. I'm coming with you and Buck is my protection. Just in case the killer returns to the scene of the crime."

"I'm not going to stop you. Just don't get in the way of Brege." I entered the elevator as the door opened. Buck and Penny followed as I pushed the button for the seventh floor. We stood quietly as the elevator zoomed up. We came to a stop and the door opened. I exited the elevator as a patrol cop stopped me just outside the door.

"Do you have business on this floor, sir?" he asked politely.

I figured I would throw out a name. "I need to see Captain Brege. Is he still here?"

"He is sir, and you are?"

"Jim Richards, he'll know me."

The officer got on his radio and made a call. I could hear Brege talking, he said he'd be out shortly.

We waited until I saw Brege coming down the hall, smiling. "You just had to get in on this," he said as he approached.

"Of course. I may need details for a book. And maybe I find something that ties into the death of the author."

"I'm not against outside help. If it gets the murder solved, I'm all for it. So, if you have anything to contribute, I'm for it," Brege said with a grin.

*

Chapter 16

"I got nothing yet, just curious about this murder," I said.

Brege looked past me and said, "Hey Buck, good to see you again. Still hanging out with this guy?"

"I got nothing better to do than keep his butt out of trouble," Buck replied with a laugh.

"That will be the day," I said. "So you think this is the Hangman?" I asked Brege.

"Same M.O. and the rope is identical to the others. We didn't broadcast much about how the hangings were committed. So this isn't a copy-cat. I don't suppose you'd like to see the crime scene?"

Penny grunted, "Not really."

"Well, you can stay out here with Buck and I'll go take a peek." I turned back to Brege, "Sure, I'd like that."

Bob Moats

The ME and his men were wheeling out the gurney with the body in its standard black bag. We moved out of the way as they maneuvered the gurney into the elevator.

I followed Brege as he went back to the room. It was a very luxurious room, probably the nicest one on the floor. I was comparing it to the one Penny and I were in, this was a lot nicer. Brege pointed out where the murder took place and explained how the body was found.

"The housekeeping people came to clean up and found her on the bed. The noose tied to the head of the bed. We won't know until after the autopsy, but the ME said she was possibly raped after she died, guy must be a necrophilia freak."

That made me shiver. "The Hangman must have a good deal of money to afford this place. Doesn't the front desk have the registration of the guy? I know you can't get a room without showing plenty of I.D. now days."

"I got men checking that out, but I'll bet you a dozen donuts it's a fake identification. This guy has used a different one in every hotel he's been in. He likes the fancy and expensive ones, not some dive motel to take a hooker to."

"He must have good taste. I mean in hotels, not hookers. I suppose he paid in cash?"

"Yep, for the night. Can't get the bills separated from all the other money to get prints, and he wipes the room clean after he's done."

"What about security cameras?" I asked.

"Got a man checking on it, but he wears a baseball cap pulled low in the past videos. He's no dummy when it comes to where the cameras are."

"So you got nothing so far?"

"Not unless the CSI can come up with something. Now, the murder of the author moved the Hangman out of his safe zone, the privacy of a hotel room. He risked being caught by a witness in the public restroom. This makes me wonder what that was all about."

"Do you think it may be a copy-cat, trying to put the blame on the Hangman?" I asked.

"You'd think that, but according to forensics, the rope on the author was an identical make to the ones used in the murder of the hookers. I doubt anyone would get lucky enough to buy the exact same rope at your local hardware. We do have one small lead, all the nooses were tied backwards so forensics thinks the killer was left handed. And we don't give out that kind of detailed info to the press."

"How far are you into the author's murder case?"

"I got a couple men looking into it more. I won't object if you want to look into it too. My men are tired and overworked. I'm sure they wouldn't object either."

"Did CSI find anything in the restroom where McWilliams was killed?"

"Nope, it was a clean in and out. The hangman had to have come in behind McWilliams, threw the noose around him and dragged him to the stall. CSI did confirm he was dragged to the stall from his heel scuffs on the floor coming from the sinks. The hangman had to be strong to drag and strangle the author with the noose. If anyone came in the room, all the Hangman would have to do is close the stall door until it was safe to leave."

"Maybe I'll go back to the convention center and take a look at the restroom. Not that it will tell me anything, but it may just give me a perspective on how it was committed. Are you just about finished here?"

"Body is gone, crime scene people are finishing up. I got nothing. So I guess I'll be going home. I haven't seen my wife in a few days. At least while she's awake. You have fun and don't get yourself hung."

Big Apple Murders

We left the room, Brege went to talk to his men and I found Buck and Penny talking to a uniformed officer. Penny smiled when I came up. "Did you get your fill of the crime scene?"

"Not much to see. But the Hangman has better taste in rooms. We need to move to a nicer room."

"If the killer likes fancy rooms, I'm fine with where we're at. You can move to a nicer room," she said. "So where are we going now? You have another crime scene to go to?"

"Actually, I do. Back to the convention center. I want to check out the restroom where McWilliams was murdered and maybe talk to his publisher again."

"Why are you doing this? You weren't hired by anyone to investigate," Penny asked me. "There's no money to be made here."

"If I write a book about this, there will be money." I smiled and kissed her on the cheek.

She walked to the elevator saying, "A kiss isn't going to cut it. I want to walk around the convention looking at all the hunky authors. Buck can still guard me." The elevator door opened and she went in.

I looked to Buck and said, "You can protect the hunky authors from Penny." Buck laughed and we got in the elevator.

Outside the hotel, we found Max at the curb holding the door open for us. He must have some way of tracking our moves. Maybe he has a link to the hotel staff, like Angelo used to have when we were trying to find the killer in Vegas back when Penny and I got married.

"Thanks, Max. You must be psychic to know we were coming," I said as I waited for Buck and Penny to get in.

"Not really, Mr. Richards. Just a good network of spies," he said with a grin. Now I knew he was doing the Angelo thing. "It's good to be connected."

Yeah, mob connections I thought, but didn't say it. I got in and Max closed the door and drove us to the convention center again.

We got out of the car and I asked Max, "Are you going to be tailing us again?"

"Of course, it's my job," he said with a smirk.

"Okay, park the car and let me know you're with me. I'd rather have you nearby than spying on me."

"Got it," he said then drove the car off. We went in the center showing our passes again and Penny said she was going to wander. Buck followed her like a shadow as I went to the restrooms.

It hadn't changed, but I didn't expect it to have. The room was empty, strange for being such a busy convention. But this restroom was in the lobby and there were more restrooms in the convention hall for the people to use. I looked at the floor, but the janitorial staff must have cleaned. So, there were no scuff marks now. I went to the stall and pushed open the door. It also was clean. Since the author was strangled there would be no blood, so I didn't expect any.

As I was looking into the stall, I felt a presence of someone behind me. I brought my hand to my Glock and drew it. I turned to find Morty standing behind me.

"Crap! Morty! I could have shot you," I said as I holstered my gun.

"Nervous are we? I saw you come into the restroom so I followed you," he said looking at where I put my gun.

The restroom door opened and in came Max. He had his arm in his coat, I realized he had a gun, too.

"You okay, Mr. Richards?" he asked.

I said, "I'm good, Max. This is my publisher, my almost late publisher."

*

Chapter 17

"Jim, are you going to sign books?" Morty asked after he acknowledged Max.

"No, I'm not. You'll have to do without me."

"Okay, just wondering. Your books are selling well, so you'll have a nice royalty check in a couple months."

"I won't hold my breath." I replied.

"So good to meet you, Max. I have to get back to the girls before they steal me blind." Morty turned and went to the door and out.

"Strange man," Max said.

"So true, Max. I didn't realize you carried a gun."

"I'm Gino's driver and bodyguard, it's required that I carry a gun. For protection. Lots of people don't care for Gino, so I need to be armed in case." Max smiled and took out his gun. It was a huge, nickel plated .357 Magnum. I suppose I could get a gun like that, but it would probably pull my pants down.

"Nice to have in a gun fight. I still like my Glock."

The restroom door opened and Max slid his gun back in the holster. Three men in suits came in and were chattering away about some new book coming out.

"Let's get out of here, I've seen enough." Max and I left the restroom and entered into the convention hall. I was wondering where Penny had led Buck to. We strolled down the aisles until I saw a small crowd of people around a woman who looked suspiciously like my wife. We went over to Buck standing off the side of the crowd, and he smiled to us.

"Can't take her anywhere without gathering fans," Buck said.

"Yep, I know. Did she behave for you?"

"She was an angel. No problem at all. Did you determine anything in the restroom?"

"Nope, but I got an idea on how it went down. The killer was quick and strong to take down McWilliams. I saw him in the stall when I found him and he was a big man. The Hangman has to be another big man. Time will tell."

I saw Penny working her way through the small crowd and coming in our direction.

"So, did you get your fill of the murder scene?" she said as she came up.

"Enough for now. I don't know the victim well enough to form an opinion."

"So, you're saying that you're not finished snooping?"

"Depends."

"On what?" she asked.

"Whether you let me or not," I said with a grin.

"I don't tell you what to do. You're afraid of me, I know. So you move slowly, so not to piss me off. Am I right?"

Big Apple Murders

"Are you?" I said.

"There you go again. Grow a pair and tell me to go watch the hunky authors while you investigate."

"Okay. What you said."

"Better. Now go play P.I. and I'll explore the gene pool of writers to see how you stack up. Are you coming Buck?"

Buck looked like he wasn't sure what to do. I smiled and said, "Go."

Penny gave me a kiss and walked off, followed by Buck looking back to me. He had a worried look on his face. I waved him off.

I turned to Max, "Well, shall we go beat some info out of a few people."

"Now you're in my backyard," Max said back with a wry grin. It sort of frightened me, not knowing how far this mob guy would go. "Okay, follow me." I headed back to Lipscott Publishing's booth.

I saw Brandon Lipscott at the table hawking the dead author's books. I stopped short of the table and listened. He was spreading the murder of the author really thick. It made me wonder if he was in on the murder to make a lot of money from the writer's death.

The crowd thinned out and I took the opportunity to move up to the table. Lipscott looked up and recognized me.

"Mr. Richards. Are you here to see how well the book sales are going?" he asked.

"I'm just seeing how well you picked the body clean before burying the bones. I'm wondering if you needed to do away with McWilliams to further your sales?"

"I resent that Richards. I had nothing to do with his death. You are very wrong. McWilliams was a friend of mine and I'm trying to make some money for his family. He'd want that."

"Family?"

"Yes, a wife and five-year-old son who won't be able to see his daddy again. I want him to remember his father as a good man." He paused then said, "Look, I know you are writer and a P.I., so I'd like to hire you to find out who did this. Just so his family can get some closure."

"You don't trust the police to find out who killed him?" I asked.

"I don't think the cops care. They have more pressing issues in this city to take care of than one writer. You're the only person who is questioning me about this. I can see you have an interest in this. So help me."

I had to mull it over. "I'll see what I can do, no promises. If I find the killer, we'll talk about hiring me and fees. If I don't, then you won't spend any money. How's that?"

"I guess I can't ask for more. Thank you, Mr. Richards. If you ever want to drop Morty, let me know."

"It's a thought. I'll be in touch," I said and motioned to Max to leave.

We left the booth and went to the section where my books were being sold. Morty was gone and the bubble headed girls were manning the sales. Max was looking at one of my books.

"I should read one of your books," Max said.

I picked up a copy of my first book and wrote on the title page, *'To Max, may you rule the world one day, Jim Richards.'* Then I handed it to him. He looked surprised and said thank you.

I looked to the next booth and saw author Dick Lawrence signing his books. Dick was with my publisher, Morty, for longer than I was, by about two years. He was a big seller for the firm and his sales were usually better than mine. But I wasn't jealous. Not much.

"Hey, Dick, how's sales?" I asked him as I moved to his table. He looked up and was surprised to see me.

"Jim, good to see you. I'm doing great. Aren't you going to sign books?" he said.

"I already did my time. I'm not fond of it. But if it sells books I guess I should do it more."

"I hate sitting here," he said and stood, apologizing to the people waiting for his book. He said he'd be back but needed to take a break. He came around the table to me. "Actually, I'm glad to see you. Can we go somewhere to talk?"

"Sure, follow me." I took him behind his booth to where Morty was stashing the extra books. Max followed me closely. I felt safe with him around. Like I was when I first met Angelo. I guess it's good to have the mob protecting you.

We were in the back and I turned to Dick and said, "What's up?"

"How are your book sales doing?" he asked.

"Uh, good, I guess. My royalties are still coming, when Morty remembers to send them."

"Yeah, that's my problem, too. I think I should be getting better than I am. But I have no real proof, yet," Dick said.

"Yet? Do you have something I may need to know about our royalties?"

"Not sure, but I'll need some help soon. Can I count on you?"

"Sure, if you have something that affects both of us, I'm ready to talk." I said.

We heard a voice from the front, it was Morty. He was not happy that Dick wasn't at the table. We left the back and came out to Morty.

"Relax, you little shit. I needed a break. You can ask me nicely to sign books, but it's not in my contract." Dick said.

Morty cringed when Dick came down on him. I usually gave Morty grief whenever I could. He wasn't a nice person, but he could be when he wanted something.

"Okay, Dick, I understand, you need rest. Do what you have to and then help sell books."

Dick got up in Morty's face and said, "Morty, I may have something to confront you with. So be ready."

"Don't worry, Dick, I'll be ready. Will you be?"

*

Chapter 18

It sounded like a threat coming from Morty to Dick. The two of them just stared at each other for a moment, and then Morty turned away. "I have to go check on the girls in Richard's booth. We'll talk later." He walked out of Dick's booth and went around the corner to mine.

"I used to think Morty was a decent guy, but the last year he's been a little odd acting. And mean." Dick said. "I confronted him once about my royalties and he nearly bit my head off. I should be getting what I'm owed, but how do I tell? I can't get Ross Willows to let me look at the accounting books, he's in charge and he doesn't like authors. Strange for him to be in the business and kicking the people who pay him."

Big Apple Murders

"I met Willows once," I said. "I didn't like him right off. I had the same problem about royalties. I questioned him and he acted like I didn't trust his work. Well, I don't. I wanted to see my account and how many books had sold, he blew me off and said not to worry. That worried me."

"I may have some info that will help both of us and other authors in our firm. I can't say yet, I'm not ready to prove anything, so I'll let you know when I'm ready and you can help."

Dick looked like he had something heavy on his mind. I let him have his space.

"Anything you need, don't be afraid to ask. I've put a lot of work into my books and I expect to get my just returns on them. Let me know," I said. I turned to Max, still standing close by and said, "Shall we go see how my booth is doing? Talk later, Dick." Max and I went over to my booth and found Morty was not there.

"Where did Morty go this time?" I asked Shelly, who was still hawking my books.

"He didn't say where, he just said that he'd be back later," she replied.

I looked to Max, "He's acting stranger than he usually does. I have a feeling he's up to something."

"You want I should have some of the boys take him in and question him?" Max said with a smile.

I immediately pictured Morty tied to a chair as mob enforcers worked him over. "No Max, thanks. I think he'll slip and let us know what he's doing. He's never been really bright, but he has a good mind for business. He started the publishing firm from nothing, now he has me and about ten other authors, he's made his mark in the business."

"I can still have him looked into, his business dealings and finances, if you'd like," Max said seriously.

I figured he could. "Well, as long as it's not illegal."

"Hey, don't look a gift horse in the butt. You may not like the smell."

He was still serious, so I tried not to laugh. "If you think it will help, I'm good with it."

Max gave me a wry smile and said, "I'll take care of it."

I heard my name being called and turned to see Mrs. Nixon coming up the aisle. "Mr. Richards, so good to see you again. Are you getting all psyched up for your speech tomorrow night?"

"Well, not exactly psyched up, but I'll be ready," I replied.

"Where is your friend Buck?"

"He's still on bodyguard duty for my wife. I don't trust all these writers around her." Actually, I was more worried about the writers. Penny could get carried away easily.

"These writers are all pussycats. They would never hurt your wife."

"True, maybe. But after the murder yesterday, I'm not letting her out alone."

"Yes, that was a tragic thing. Poor Mr. McWilliams. It just isn't right."

"Murder never is," I said.

"Yes, and you have seen your share of murder, haven't you?"

"Just short of a police detective, I've seen my share. You don't have any idea who may have wanted to kill him?"

"Oh, goodness no. I hardly knew the man, other than by reputation. There are just too many writers out there to know each one," she said.

I looked past her and could see down the aisle that Morty was talking to Ross Willows, his company accountant. They seemed to be arguing, or at least disagreeing on something. I really wanted to hear what they were saying. I excused myself from Mrs. Nixon. "I'm sorry, but I see someone I have to talk to. Excuse us."

I signaled to Max and we left Mrs. Nixon with her mouth opened. I walked carefully down to where I was behind a large sign announcing a book release, and stood behind it. I was close to the two men so, I listened. Max waited behind me.

"I don't know how much trouble he can start, but we need to be careful." Morty was saying.

"Well, it needs to be taken care of. I'll work with my man and see that it goes no further," Willows said. Willows then turned and left Morty standing by himself.

I came around the sign and was going to Morty when he took off, moving quickly away. I stopped and watched him go.

"You sure you don't want me to have him questioned?" Max said behind me. I don't think he knew what was going on but, he sensed something wasn't kosher.

"Thanks Max. I want to first find out what he is up to. Then you can have him," I said.

Max cracked his knuckles in one movement and it was loud. It startled me. I crack my knuckles occasionally, but never that loud.

"I'll wait for you to turn him loose then," he said with a grin.

I was glad Max was aware something was going on. I didn't know how far to let Max in on this, or how far he would go. You can't tell the mob what to do, so I would just throw little pieces to Max and see just how far.

"You said you could access his financials and maybe his criminal activities?" I asked.

"I already made a call. I can let you know as soon as my people call me," he said.

"You're full of surprises. Shall we go see what my wife and Buck are up to?"

He nodded and I pulled my cell phone. Buck answered after a couple rings and said, "Hey, Jimmy, what's up?"

"Just wondering what trouble you two are getting into?"

"We're over by the stage. They're going to have some woman talk about her erotica books. I'm all over that."

"Max and I will join you shortly. We're still exploring the crime. Later," I said and hung up.

I was looking around the area, and led Max back to my booth. The bubble-headed girls were still pushing my books. I asked Shelly where Morty was.

"I haven't seen him in over an hour, he was supposed to come back and count books," she replied.

We were standing there when we heard a scream from nearby. I turned to the sound and went in that direction, followed by Max. It came from the booth of Dick Lawrence. The two girls who were selling his books were standing just outside the booth looking shocked. One of the girls was crying. I came up and asked what was wrong. The crying girl pointed to the booth. I looked there and didn't see anything, so asked, "What?"

"In the back," she stammered. I went into the booth and looked through the curtain to the back and saw him. Dick Lawrence was lying on the floor with a noose around his neck. He definitely looked dead.

Chapter 19

Brege was not happy to be back at the book convention and said so.

"Do all the murder writers actually murder people to be able to write their stories?" he asked. "And why are you always around while this is going on?" he said to me.

"It's my curse, remember?"

"Oh, yeah. I'll need to talk to your wife about that. Maybe you're murdering people to have something to write about."

"I have no defense, except I have alibis for every murder. I like to keep people around me so I can verify that I murdered no one."

"You're too clever. I'm keeping my eye on you. Now tell me what you know about this."

I smiled and said, "Well, Max and I were standing by my booth when we heard a scream."

"Max?" Brege asked.

I pointed to Max, who was standing in the aisle. Brege looked over to him and grunted. "Are you still hanging with the Traviano family?"

"No, they seem to be hanging with me. Max is driving my wife and me around the city."

"Is that all he's doing?"

"I'm his alibi, too," I said with a grin.

"Now I don't trust either of you. Especially Mad Max."

"Mad Max?"

"I got stories I can tell you when he's not around." Brege said with a grin also.

"Should I worry?"

"Nah, you're a friend of the Travianos, so I'm sure you're safe."

"That's comforting. I'm a friend of a mob family, so I'm protected. Shouldn't I expect that from the police?"

"We're too busy to worry about you. So enjoy your friendship with the mob," he said with a loud laugh. When he calmed, he asked, "Okay, so what happened?"

I gave a watered down version of my adventure in the center. I didn't get into the Morty – Willows incident, that was my business and I didn't need to share it right now. Although I felt I should bring up that fact as Morty had a problem with Dick Lawrence. I knew Morty didn't have the stomach for murder. Maybe Willows killed Dick. Should I let Brege know?

"Richards, you're thinking too heavily. You got something to tell me?" Brege said.

"My publisher had a disagreement with the victim just before he was murdered. I'm ninety-nine percent sure he didn't do it, but if you want to talk to him, it may be worth it." I was giving Brege a small bit of info. It may help.

"You know where your publisher is?"

"At this moment, no. My sales girls said he would be back, but he was gone around the time of the murder."

"Coroner said the vic was murdered around the time you found him. Fresh kill," he said. "The Hangman had to have lured Lawrence into the back and strangled him quickly. There's not a lot of room back there, so he has to be strong to keep him from struggling around."

I was glancing around the area to see if I could see a big man looking like he wasn't interested in books. All I was seeing was Max. I knew he didn't do it, but he may know something about the Hangman. I excused myself from Brege, who went back to the crime scene. I went to Max.

"Max, do you know anyone who goes by the nickname of the Hangman?" I asked.

"Doesn't sound familiar," Max said. "If you're talking about a hitman who strangles people with a rope, I know a couple."

"This one has been taking down hookers on a regular basis. Now he may have murdered two authors."

"Hookers? That's not nice. I'll put out the word to watch for this guy."

"That may help. I'm sure you have a pipeline to the other families who may know something," I said.

"I got ears all over the place. I may be Gino's personal driver and bodyguard, but I have been in this business as long as he has, and he knows it. As I got older, Gino gave me some easy jobs to do. I used to be a real hell raiser in my day. Got a few skeletons in my closet."

I didn't want to ask. Brege could fill me in on the dirt about Max later. I heard a voice behind me and cringed. It was Penny.

"More murders! Are you trying to beat your previous score?" she said loudly.

"I have no previous score."

"Do you want me to give you a rundown of your past?"

"No, thank you," I said.

"So what happened?" she asked.

"Dick Lawrence. He was murdered behind his booth."

"Okay, so you are to stay away from the restrooms and your booth. Anywhere else you could be murdered?"

"No, that pretty much covers it."

Penny looked to the booth where they were taking the body out. "Did you know this author?"

"I was talking to him not long before he died. I didn't know him real well, but he was a nice guy. Something is not right here. He said he had some info regarding our royalties, now he's gone."

"Royalties? Why would anyone kill for royalties?" she asked.

"If there are enough writers selling books, the money could add up to a fortune if skimmed off from each. But it would have to be some creative book cooking to get away with it. I don't really know how much I make until I'm told by the accountants. They could skim off a lot of money from all of us and it would never be found out."

"Isn't there ways to tell how many books you've sold?"

"Our firm controls the book sales and reports what they want. I don't like it and I've thought about changing my connections with Morty."

"I've never liked the man. He just seems sneaky to me," Penny said with a grin.

I looked to Buck and said, "You're being awful quiet about this."

"I'm not taking sides. I have to put up with the both of you." Buck said.

"Put up? Buck, do you put up with me?" Penny asked.

I really think Buck turned pale. He cleared his throat and said, "No, Penny, not put up. I have to…uh…well, I need to deal with both of you. I don't like to take sides."

"Smart man," I said.

Brege came up, "Hello, Mrs. Richards. How are you?"

"I'm fine. Have you caught the killer yet? My husband probably did it."

"I'm watching him, thanks. My wife was excited that I came in contact with you during this case. She watches your show every day. Can I get an autograph for her? It would give me a little credibility with her."

"Of course. Maybe tomorrow I could come by and say hi to her?" Penny asked.

"Well, that would elevate me to sainthood. I don't want you to go out of your way."

"No problem. It may help my husband get a lighter sentence for murder," Penny said with a grin.

"I'll consider it. Now, if you'll excuse me, I have to investigate. Do some real cop stuff." He saluted her and went off.

"I like that man," Penny said. "You should be more like him."

"What, a big black man with an attitude for killing people in organized crime?" I said as I looked to where Max had been standing. He wasn't there now.

I turned to see if I could spot Max, but he was gone. I wasn't worried about him, but it was strange he just went off.

"Shall we go get something to eat?" Penny asked.

"I'm good for that. Shall we go?" I said. We were heading to the exit when Max came up from somewhere, I didn't know. He was sneaky.

"Max, you disappeared," I said.

Max was serious, "I got a call, went to get some privacy. I need to talk to you about your publisher. He has some things to hide."

*

Chapter 20

I was a bit stunned by Max's remark. "Okay, let's talk," I said and looked to Penny.

"Go investigate. Buck and I can go get something to eat. You okay with being my husband for a while?" she said to Buck. He turned pale again and looked at me.

"Go," I said and waved them off. Buck grinned and took Penny out of the center. I turned back to Max and said, "Let's go find some place comfortable. Or is this going to be short?"

Max grinned, "Nope. Got a lot to tell you."

"Okay, follow me," I said and led him to my booth. We passed Shelly, who was still pushing my books. I felt funny going to the back of the booth, the area where Dick was murdered three booths over. I felt safe with Max for obvious reasons. I hoped his age hadn't slowed down his trigger finger. But my finger worked just fine.

I checked around for anyone hiding in the back and found no one. I pulled up a chair for Max and I sat on a short stack of book boxes.

"Okay, what did you find?" I asked.

"I called my people and gave them your publisher's name and his connection to his company. They did their magic and dug into his affairs and found he wasn't a good boy."

I sat waiting. Max was being dramatic.

"It seems Morty has a lot of money stashed in some off-shore account. More than would have been earned in a lifetime for most people. Rich people that is." He reached in his jacket pocket and brought out a note pad. He glanced at it and then said, "He was investing heavily in Mortimer Shay Productions, a theatre production company."

"Morty did have a couple playwrights in his firm. He may have been banking on producing their plays. Maybe starting his own theatre company."

"Except there is no company. He fronted a shell company and had no building or business. It seems that Morty has other ventures also. He has plans to open a string of bagel stands, "Morty's Better Bagels" and a spa for men with a gym. All on paper, no businesses."

"Okay, he's sneaky with his money and starting fake companies. Does that make him bad or in trouble?"

"He's in debt to some loan sharks."

"I thought he has money hidden away?"

"He does and yet he needs more. There's something going on and no one is talking. I had my people dig and he has a partner. No name yet, but they're still digging."

I thought for a moment. "What would this have to do with the death of Dick Lawrence?"

"I was listening to what you had to say earlier. If your publisher was skimming money and Lawrence had some proof, murder would be an answer to keep him silent."

"I can't see Morty murdering anyone."

"You have a serial killer murdering authors. Maybe the first killing was a mistake or a way to distract from what Lawrence knew. Either way, this Hangman you mentioned is working for someone close to the authors."

"If Dick Lawrence had some proof that Morty was skimming royalties, then it would be a good reason to kill him. But again, Morty isn't that devious. Now I can see Ross Willows, the accountant, doing something like that. Can you get anything on him?"

"I'll call my people and see." Max stood and pulled his cell phone. He made a call and then hung up. "They'll get back to me as soon as they have something."

"Thanks Max, I appreciate all this."

"No problem, Mr. Richards. You've been a good friend to Angelo and the rest of the family. We take care of our friends."

"You know, for a wiseguy, you're okay," I said with a grin, hoping he took it as a compliment.

"For a fake cop you're not bad yourself. Shall we go see what your wife and friend are doing?"

I laughed and got up off the stack of book boxes. We went out and ran into Morty, who was standing in my booth next to the bubble-headed girls. "Jim, how long have you been back there?" he asked.

I wondered if he was listening to us in the back. The room was noisy enough to cover what we were saying but, if he got close enough to the curtain between the front and the back, he could possibly hear us.

"We were discussing business. This person is with another publishing company trying to take me away from you." I lied for a good reason.

Big Apple Murders

"Oh, what company?" Morty asked.

"Lifton Publishing," Max said, without blinking an eye. I wondered how he pulled that out of the air. Lifton was a big New York publisher, sought out by many writers.

"Lifton? Well, I guess we have to talk, Jim. I'll call you," he said and left the booth.

"Lifton? How did you come up with that name?" I asked Max.

Max smiled, "The family has their hands in a number of legit businesses. Lifton is owned by a shell company run by Gino. It's one reason he has a fondness for writers, like yourself. If you want to jump ship on Morty, I'm sure Lifton would love to take you on."

"I'll think on it." I was amazed by the connections from Gino to my life. I'd have to have a talk with Angelo when I got back home.

"Do you think Morty may have heard us talking?" I asked.

"If he did, he's going to have to do something to silence you and me. He doesn't know my connections to the family?"

"No, he hardly knows you and hasn't asked me about you. What we discussed in the back, he could think you are a cop investigating him. So, if he's going to whack us, he better do it quickly and carefully."

"I can have some of my men watch him."

"No, I think we can handle it. If the situation gets bad, you can bring in your army with my blessings."

"You got it. Shall we go find your people?"

I pulled my cell phone and called Penny. She came on after two rings. "You're too late, Buck and I just eloped," she said.

"Good, he can take care of you now," I replied.

"Are you finished investigating?"

"For now, yes. Where are the two of you?"

"Some Italian restaurant down the street from the center. Are you coming?"

"The name?"

She asked someone the name of the restaurant, and then said, "Linguini's. Isn't that some kind of food?"

"Yes, it's pasta. Max and I will find it. Be there shortly," I said and hung up.

I told Max the name of the place and he laughed. "I've eaten there before. Follow me."

We left and took a nice walk down the street. The day was starting to get dim. I figured since there were so many huge and high buildings, the sun didn't get down here unless it was directly overhead. We arrived at the restaurant and went in. I saw Penny and Buck at a table by the window and we joined them. I could see they already ate.

"Is the food good here?" I asked.

"Fantastic, just like Angelo's restaurant. Only more expensive here. Good thing I'm using the firm's credit card," she said with a grin.

I wondered if there would be any money left in my account by the time Penny got done in New York.

*

Chapter 21

We finished eating and I grabbed the credit card from Penny. She wasn't happy.

"I don't want to go broke before we get back," I said.

"You have more money than the Pope. Why are you worrying?"

"At least I don't go around wearing a tall pointy hat while sitting on a throne of gold."

"It's not gold. Now what are we going to do?"

I looked at Max and said, "What do you suggest we do now?"

Max grinned and replied, "I'm not the best social director you can pick. But I can think of a real nice karaoke bar I could take you to."

Penny was bouncing. "Karaoke! Let's go there."

Big Apple Murders

I wasn't fond of karaoke, but if it made Penny happy, I'd agree. "Okay Max, are you going to sing too?"

"I do a great Sinatra impersonation," he said with a big grin.

"That, I want to see," I said as my cell phone buzzed.

"If that call is about another murder, I'm murdering you," Penny said to me.

The caller ID said it was private, but I answered. "Hello?"

The voice on the phone said, "If you want to know who murdered your author friends, go out of your restaurant, turn right, go two blocks. I'll find you. Come alone." The caller hung up.

I looked to Penny, she didn't smile. "It was someone saying they would tell me who murdered the authors. I have to go down the block to meet them."

Max said, "You're not going alone."

"He said I had to."

Max was silent, then said, "I can go out first and across the street to watch you."

Bob Moats

"No Max, take Penny to the karaoke bar and Buck can follow me."

Penny said, "Like hell, I'm not going to let you go get killed too. Buck and I can go across the street and look like a couple. Less suspicious that way. Max can come up behind us."

I thought on it and said, "Okay. You go out first then I come out shortly. Be careful, the caller knew I was in this restaurant. So he knows I'm with you guys."

"Buck and Penny can go out front. I know a way on this street from the back. I'll be nearby." Max got up and went towards the back of the restaurant and disappeared into the kitchen.

I turned back to Buck and said, "You keep Penny safe, but watch me. Not closely, or whoever this person is will know."

"You got it. I'll watch you like a hawk," Buck said as he and Penny stood. "We'll be across the street."

"Have your gun ready," I said as they headed out. Buck said he had his hand on it.

I sat wondering who the mysterious caller was. I felt very alone. The waitress came and took my card to pay for the meals. I waited until she came back, gave her a generous tip, and stood. I figured whoever the caller was would wait.

I walked out the door and turned right. The street was dark and had only a few people wandering about. There were a couple restaurants and bars on the street, so there were people. I hoped the caller wouldn't open fire, some innocent persons could be hurt. I took my Glock off safety and was ready to use it. I didn't like going in blind on a call like this. I had no idea what to expect.

I counted two blocks and stood on the corner waiting to be approached. I wished I had my bulletproof vest. I didn't pack it because I didn't think any of the writers would shoot me. I'll have to rethink packing it next time.

I glanced across the street and could barely see Penny and Buck slowly walking on the sidewalk. It was dark on their side, which was good. I had no idea where Max was.

I stood waiting, when I heard a voice behind me. It chilled my bones.

"Richards, come into the alley," the voice said.

"Oh, hell no. You can come out here. There's no one on the street who will disapprove of your activities. And I'm not about to be shot."

The man was in shadows so I couldn't see him very well. I could hear him moving about, he seemed nervous.

"Look, you said on the phone that you knew who murdered the authors. Just tell me and we'll be done. You can go hide in the darkness and I can go nab the killer," I said.

"Maybe I murdered the authors, what would you say to that?" the mysterious voice said.

"Well, if you did, you killed with a noose, and I'm not going to let you put one around my neck."

The stranger was silent.

"You didn't know the men were killed with a noose, did you? Do you really know who killed the men?"

"Shut up and get into the alley," he said, and I could see a gun sticking out from the shadows.

"Ah, now it begins. So what is it? The theft of royalties from the authors? Embezzlement is the term. Did Morty send you, or are you Morty?"

"Stop talking and get into the alley!" he yelled now.

I didn't move, hoping he wouldn't shoot me out here. It was suddenly quiet in the alley, then I saw a man coming out with Max right behind him. A very big magnum at the stranger's head.

"You want I should shoot him, Mr. Richards? I can dump him in the East River," Max said.

I was trying not to laugh. "No, I think Captain Brege may want to talk to him. Then you can shoot him."

Buck and Penny came up behind me, causing me to jump.

"Nervous, sweetie?" Penny said.

"Me? Never." I turned back to the man. I didn't recognize him. "Talk to me or I'll have my friend dump you in the East River."

The man stood quietly, but looked a little nervous.

"I don't know you. Who sent you?" I asked.

He didn't say anything. Max took hold of his arm and twisted it behind him, causing the man pain. I probably should have stopped Max, but hey, he's a mob man, he does what he wants. I saw Max whisper something in the man's ear and the man turned pale.

"I can't say who sent me, I don't know. I was hired through a website to take you out. No names, just payment and information on the hit."

"Hitman?" I heard Penny say. "This must be a big deal for them to send a hitman for you."

"Do you always pick up your hits through this website. What's it called?"

He said nothing. Max squeezed his arm and he yelled, "HitmenforHire.com."

"Do you know a man named Morty Shay?" I asked him.

The man didn't respond. "How about Ross Willows?"

That got a small response. He flinched.

"Is Willows behind the killings?"

No response again.

"Okay, how about the Hangman, you know him?" I asked.

This time the man looked totally spooked. "No, take me in to jail. I demand protection."

Penny spoke, "Well, a hitman afraid of another killer. That's scary."

I agreed with her, pulled my cell phone out and called Brege. When he answered, I said, "You're going to hate me for this."

*

Chapter 22

Brege had called for a patrol car to pick up the perp. We followed to the precinct in the town car and were escorted to Brege's office. I was surprised to see him in a tuxedo.

"Do you always dress formally for late night questioning?" I asked.

He grinned and said, "You saved me from having to put up with stuffy snobs at a very boring event for the local library. I'm all for the library, but the people who run it are all blowhards."

Penny and I were in Brege's office, Buck and Max decided to stay out by the car. Neither of them had a liking for the police, especially Max. I turned to see a very attractive black woman enter the room. She was dressed in an evening gown and lots of jewelry.

Brege put his arm around her and said, "Jim, Penny, this is my wife, Althea. Baby, you know who Penny is. I hope you two don't mind, you called while we were at the event and my wife heard where I was going and who I was seeing and she insisted on coming along."

Penny moved to the woman and held her hand out. They shook and Althea said, "When Lou told me he was meeting you two here, I had to come. So good to meet you. Even under the circumstances. Let's go out in the squad room and let the men beat their chests."

Penny laughed out loud. "I'm going to like you," she said as they went out of the room.

"Okay, P.I., what's the story?" he asked me.

I watched Penny and Althea go to the far side of the squad room and sit. I looked to Brege and told him about the call at the restaurant. I explained how we separated and went to the area where I was told to go. I didn't say that Max had a gun on the hitman, I said he subdued the man.

"With a gun, right?" Brege asked.

I smiled, "Would it make a difference?"

"Max is a bodyguard and he has a license to carry, so I'll ignore the fact. Now what did the perp say to you?"

I went over the facts as best I could remember as Brege sat nodding.

"So, he admitted to you he was hired to take you out?" Brege asked.

"Yep, not a pleasant conversation, but that's what he was hired to do."

"How are you hooked up with the other two authors and why wasn't the Hangman involved?"

"I don't know. This weasel had a handgun and no ropes. Maybe the person who hired the Hangman couldn't get him to do the job." I said. "So he hired this guy."

"I'll look into this website, HitmanforHire.com. I've never heard of it before. He could be lying."

"It could be a blocked website, one that needs a password to get in," I said.

"I'll have our tech people check it out. As long as this guy pulled a gun on you and you have witnesses, we can hold him." Brege turned to the women outside the office. "I hope my wife doesn't talk your wife's ear off. She does that to me. I just tune her out and nod my head. She never questions it."

"Penny loves to yank my chain by changing subjects in mid-sentence. I have to pay attention to her. Are you going to question him?"

"As soon as he's booked. I told my men to put him in interrogation. Since you were the almost victim and sort of know what's going on, I'll let you sit in. Maybe make the perp nervous or say something he shouldn't."

"Be glad to help."

"He should be ready by now, let's go." Brege went out, followed by me, and then he stopped. "Althea," he called to his wife. She looked over to us. "I'm going to beat up a suspect. Don't you two get in any trouble." He moved to a hallway and through a couple doors until we came to a door marked 'Interrogation 2' and went in.

The cop watching the man handed Brege a large envelope, then left the room. Brege opened the envelope and pulled out a paper from inside. He read it and glanced at the perp, "Well, Isaac, you are in a bit of trouble," he said, putting the envelope on the table. He sat and motioned to me to the chair by the door. I pulled the chair over and sat.

"We got you for attempted murder, confessing to being a hitman, and I'll throw in being ugly. Who hired you?"

Isaac sat saying nothing.

"You're going to go down, Isaac. May as well take someone with you."

"I told the P.I. all I know, nothing. I got the info from the website in an email, and went to do the job. I never know who hires me." Isaac said.

Brege picked up the envelope and reached inside. He brought out a cell phone and examined it.

"Is that email on this phone?" Brege asked.

Isaac got a look on his face and said, "I guess it is."

"You guess? You don't know how to operate your phone?"

"Yeah, okay. It's on there."

Bob Moats

Brege was pushing buttons and then smiled. "Okay, I found your email program. You didn't password protect it. Bad for you." He studied it for a bit then looked to me. "Seems you weren't the only person to be hit. Max was listed in this email."

I immediately thought of Morty and the incident in the booth. I was sure he heard us talking. "Hey Brege, I need to talk to you about something that happened earlier, after I last saw you."

"I don't think we need to talk to Isaac anymore, but we may have more questions later." He waved to the cop outside the door and he came in. "Take our friend here to a nice cold cell."

The cop took Isaac away as Brege and I left the room. He went back to his office and we sat. Penny and Althea were still having an animated conversation, both laughing and smiling. I was glad Penny had a female to talk to. Buck and I tried our best to keep her happy, but it's not the same.

"Okay, what do you have?" Brege asked.

I told him about the conversation Max and I had. I told him about the shady dealings Morty was doing and that it was very possible that Morty heard us talking. "Good reason to silence us, so we wouldn't expose him. Dick Lawrence told me he had some information on a possible embezzling of our royalties. At least that's what I got out of the

171

conversation. Then Dick ended up dead. Now Max and I are next to die."

"I'll need to bring in your publisher and this accountant. Do you know where to find them?"

"Nope, but I'm sure they aren't far from the convention. At least Morty will be there watching his money. He can lead you to the accountant." I looked at my watch. "The convention is closing down so, you may have to find him in the morning. He wouldn't have any idea whether Isaac completed the hit on Max and me or not. So, I don't think he'll be in hiding. I don't know where he lives or I'd take you there."

Brege yelled for someone named Harris. A man came in the room and said, "What ya need, Captain?"

"See if you can track down a man." He looked to me and asked the name. I told him. "Okay, find this Morty Shay and bring him in for questioning."

"You got it boss," Harris said and left.

"The plot thickens," Brege said to me.

*

Chapter 23

We went over to where the women were enjoying themselves. Penny smiled at me and said, "Jim, Althea invited me to her home tomorrow for lunch. You don't mind?"

"No, have fun. I'm sure Buck, Max, and I can find something to do." I replied.

"Chase criminals, mostly," Penny said with a grin.

"That too. I may even get Morty arrested for murder."

"Now, that I would like to see." Penny said happily.

We were interrupted by Harris. "I think we got a lock on where Shay is living. I'm taking a couple men to bring him in."

"Put him in holding until the morning. Tell him he's a suspect in a murder investigation," Brege said. "That should make him worry."

"Or give him time to work up an alibi," I said.

"We'll beat the truth out of him," Brege said.

"You really enjoy your job don't you?" I asked.

"Harris!" Brege yelled to the man as he was heading out of the squad room.

"Yeah, Captain?"

Brege asked me the name of the accountant. I told him.

"Harris, when you have Shay in custody, ask him where you can find Ross Willows. Bring him in, too. May as well make a party out of it."

"Sure, Captain." He went off again.

"Well, I'm worn out. Althea, you have a long day tomorrow entertaining your guest. Let's go home and get some sleep," Brege said.

"That's all you do, Lou, is sleep. But it has been a busy day for me, too. Penny, I'll have Lou send a car to pick you up and we can have lunch."

"Works for me," Penny said and stood. "We need to get some rest, too. Don't we, sweetie?"

"I didn't get my nap today. I'm ready for bed," I said.

We said our good-byes and went out to the parking lot. Buck was sitting on the hood of the car and Max was sitting next to him. They both looked happy.

"Time to go back to the hotel. Oh, and Max, you were mentioned in the hit also. We missed the big score," I said.

"I'll have to talk to my people and see what this is about." Max said.

"I think we got it pretty much figured out." I said. "Morty is being arrested as we speak and Willows is not far behind."

"You think they murdered the authors?" Buck asked.

"No, but they probably set it up. I know that Dick had something on Morty. I don't know about the first author. He may have been collateral damage. Wrong place, wrong time."

"But you and Max are scheduled to die, aren't you worried?" Buck asked.

"I've been scheduled to die a lot of times. But you, Penny, Earl, Trapper, and my Glock have prevented it. Now, we have Max and his Magnum. I'm not worried."

"I'll take you to the hotel and hang around the lobby," Max said.

"You don't need to do that," I said.

"Max, you can bunk in with me," Buck offered.

"I'd like that, Buck, thanks."

We all piled into the car and Max drove us over to the hotel. We got out and Buck told Max what room he was in. Max said after he parked, he'd be up. Buck, Penny, and I went up in the elevator and the door opened to our floor. Buck went to his room and Penny followed me to ours. I got to the suite door and found it was not locked.

I signaled to Penny and whispered to go get Buck. She went down the hall and tapped on his door quietly. I saw them whispering and Buck came down the hall with his .38 out. I had my Glock ready for whatever was behind the door. I stood to the side of the door and pushed it slowly open. There were no shots fired, so I started to enter after whispering to Penny to wait outside. She already had her Smith & Wesson out.

I entered the room carefully as it was dark. I remember leaving a light on, but it was out. I reached for the room switch on the wall, it didn't work. Damn, this was not good. Buck moved around me with his gun out in front of him. The light from the hallway was all we had in the room. I pulled the small flashlight on my keychain and turned it on. The thing was small but powerful. It lit the room in front of me. I saw nothing.

I heard a noise from our left and then heard the blast from the gun in the dark. Buck spun around and went down. I brought my gun up and fired into the darkness at whoever was there. I saw someone running for the door and would have fired, but Penny was standing in the hallway with her gun out. I didn't want to hit her. The man raised his weapon and Penny fired three shots into his chest. He went down.

Max came running up as I went to turn on a lamp on the table. Max jumped over the body of our intruder and went right to Buck. He had blood coming from his arm. Not a lot, Max said it was a flesh wound. Buck looked up and asked if we got him. I grinned and said Penny did.

A half hour later, Brege was pacing the suite room and was not happy. "I want you in protective custody until we can weed out all these hitmen."

Max cleared his throat. "I put a call into Gino and we will have a number of men here shortly. No one will get through them."

Brege stared at Max, then smiled. "Okay, I'm going to overlook the fact that these men are part of a

crime family. As long as they don't break the law."
He looked at me. "Is Buck alright?"

"The hotel doctor is in his room with him. He
says he'll live. Just a scratch. This hitman wasn't a
very good shot."

"Well, we can write him off our list of bad
guys." He turned to Penny. "You are one hell of a
good sharp shooter, girl. Nice shot grouping. All in
the heart."

"Don't underestimate my wife's ability with a
gun. She's saved the day many times."

"Think you'll get some sleep now?" Brege
asked, grinning.

"I'll be up all night. Even with the mob
watching us."

"A least I don't have to pay overtime for my
men." Brege said. "I guess Morty and Willows are
desperate to silence you. They don't know we know.
Well, maybe Morty does know, now that he's in
custody."

"I wonder how many hitmen they hired?"

"Doesn't matter with the mob watching you
now. I have to follow the body out and file my report.
I'll need you to come in tomorrow morning to give a

statement. Oh, and I'll have a patrol car come to pick up your wife to visit mine. I'll say it's protective custody."

"I'll be sure she's ready and send a couple of Gino's men with her."

"My wife will love that," Brege said with a laugh. "See you in the morning." He walked out of the room leaving Penny and me alone. Max was at the door and said he'd be there until his men came. He closed the door and I turned to Penny.

"Well, it's been a quiet day, huh?"

She gave me the finger, then laughed.

*

Chapter 24

Penny was asleep in the bed, while I sat on an easy chair in the living area with the TV on low. I heard a slight tapping on the door and went over to it. I peeked through the spy hole and saw it was Max. I opened the door.

"Max, what's up?" I said as two very huge, mean looking men came up on both sides of Max. It startled me at first, then I realized they were Gino's men. "Well, the Cavalry has arrived."

"You got it, Mr. Richards. This is Louis and Salvatore. They'll be out here covering your door," Max explained.

"Thank you, men. I feel safe already." I said, grinning. "Max, have you seen Buck?"

"Yeah, he's not happy, but he's safe and won't die from lead poisoning." Max gave me a big grin. "Sleep well, we'll make sure no one gets to you and the Mrs."

I thanked them again and closed the door. I went into the bedroom suite and undressed. I was tired, but awake. I knew I had to give my speech tomorrow, so I needed to rest. I crawled under the sheets slowly so not to disturb Penny.

"I have my gun under my pillow, so no fast moves," Penny said quietly.

I held in a laugh and put my head on my pillow. "I'm in no mood to move fast tonight. Our front door has two very big men watching it." I'm not sure how fast I fell asleep, but I was dreaming of being chased by dozens of hitmen.

I heard a voice and opened my eyes. The sun was shining in the room and I was looking into the face of Gino Traviano. I just about screamed, but caught myself. He was leaning over me and said, "You need to get up. It's a beautiful day and there will be no more trouble for you and Penny."

He straightened up and turned to go out of the room. I looked over and saw that Penny was not in bed. I glanced at my watch and it was just after seven. Not my time of the day to get up. But when the capo of a mob family tells you to get up, you do it, or sleep with the fishes.

I dressed and went out to find Gino, Frances, and Penny relaxing.

"Did I miss anything?" I asked.

"You and Max really pissed off someone." Gino spoke. "I had my people look into this website for hitmen and found that there was a bounty put on both of you. So there were any number of men wanting to take you out. I had a warning put up that you were protected by my people and consequences would be dire if you did get hurt. I think that should take care of it."

I was honored that I was being protected by a crime family. "Anything as to who posted the hit?"

"I got my people checking into that. Nice that I don't need a warrant to examine the website files." Gino grinned.

"Yes, probable cause for the police to check, also."

"I talked to Lou Brege this morning, we go back a number of years. He's good people, for a cop. I told him what we found, he was grateful for the information. They have your publisher in custody, but the accountant is missing. I got people looking for him."

"You will turn him over to the police?"

Gino grinned again, "Yeah, sure."

I guess the fishes will have a swimming partner. "I have to go in to file a statement on the incident last night. Thank you for coming out and for your men to watch over us."

Gino stood and came to me. He gave me a hug and a kiss on the cheek. I hoped it wasn't the kiss of death.

"Jim, you're our friend and we respect friendship. You are part of the family now. We protect family." Gino turned to Frances and said, "Let's leave these two to their activities. We have church to go to."

182

I could imagine Gino and God talking about business. 'Hey, Gino, how's business?', 'Not bad, God, any chance I may end up there?'

Frances stood and hugged Penny, then they said their good-byes.

I saw them to the door and checked to see if the giants were still at the door, they were.

"So, did you have a nice talk with our guests?" I asked, after it was quiet in the room.

"We did, not a long talk, but nice. You made some waves out here, didn't you?"

"You know I can get in trouble just by standing still," I said, looking innocent. "I have to go make my statement and you have a lunch date."

There was a knock on the door and I looked through the peep hole. It was Buck. I opened the door and was amazed that he looked almost puny next to the door guards.

"Hey, pal, come on in. How's the arm?"

He entered, "It hurts a little, but I'll survive. Got something to brag about back home."

"At least we aren't shipping you home in a box. I'm getting ready to go see Brege and make my report. Where's Max?"

"He said he had some things to do but would meet us later. I gave him my cell phone number."

"Good, let's get some breakfast before we go out into the world to get shot at."

"Not funny," Penny said as she gathered her things to go.

We went out of the room and the two goons were right on our heels.

I was concerned about the weight limit on the elevator, but it didn't strain. We made it to the lobby safely. We went out to the street and down to a small grill that served breakfast. I invited the goons to eat, they politely refused.

We came out of the restaurant and found Max at the curb with the car. "You are sneaky aren't you?" I asked.

"Best way to be, less problems," he said.

We got in the car. One goon in front, one in back with us. Max drove us to Brege's precinct and the goons stayed with the car.

"Buck, you'll have to come in to tell your side of the story. Max, you may as well come too. You were part of this hit."

They both agreed reluctantly and we went in. The desk officer called Brege to say we were here. We waited a few minutes when Detective Harris came to get us. He led us to the homicide squad room.

"Did they find Willows yet?" I asked the detective.

"Still in the wind. We got a BOLO out for him, it will only be a matter of time," Harris replied.

Brege was standing in his office as we arrived. He was reading from a paper then turned to us. "Got something on Willows. Seems he has warrants out for embezzlement in three states. His name isn't Willows, it's Harve Rosen. That's his real name, he's had others."

"Embezzlement? What kind?"

"Mostly financial firms. He ventured into publishing here in New York. Hooked up with Morty and the rest is a subject for your books." He smiled at Penny, "I have a car waiting to take you to see my wife. May God have mercy on your soul."

"I'll tell her you said that," Penny said with a laugh.

Brege yelled for Harris and he came to the door, "Yeah, boss?"

"Take Mrs. Richards to the car I have waiting to take her to my wife."

"You got it, follow me ma'am."

Penny kissed me, "Don't get killed, you hear."

"Not with the police and the mob hovering around me." I kissed her back and she went out with Harris.

"Max, Buck, have a seat." He pointed to the side of his office. They went to sit as he pointed to a chair by his desk for me. "Boring stuff, filling out a statement on the crime, but it has to be done to make it all nice and legal." He handed me a tablet and gave one each to Max and Buck. We spent the next hour writing and talking about what happened to get our facts straight.

We finished and Brege stood. "Shall we go have a talk with your publisher? I'll let you come in, it may rattle him."

We went back to the same interrogation room the hitman was in and I looked in the window. Morty was looking miserable.

"May I beat on him a few times too?" I asked Brege.

*

Chapter 25

Morty's head snapped up when Brege blew through the door. I was behind him, and when Morty saw me, he jumped up.

"Jim, what's going on? They brought me in because they think I murdered someone."

Brege got in Morty's face and yelled to sit. Morty did.

"Okay, Shay, talk to me about skimming company funds."

Morty got a shocked look on his face. "What are you talking about?"

"Willows is an embezzler, and you hired him. You also have a whole lot of money in an off-shore account. Now, I put the two together, and you and Willows are working together. Stealing money from your authors. Dick Lawrence had you on his radar, so you had him killed."

"I don't know what you're talking about. Yes, I have money in an off-shore account, I'm not fond of paying taxes. I got the money from an inheritance. My grandfather passed and he left me his fortune."

I spoke up, "What about Morty's Bagels and the spa?"

"You found out about that? Okay, I make fake companies to shelter my money as I bring it in from the off-shore accounts. I may be a crooked businessman, but I'm not a killer."

"What about Willows?" Brege asked.

"Willows? I hired him because old man Moore, my former accountant, died last year. He came highly recommended by his former employers."

"Did you even check his references or just take his word for it?"

Morty was quiet, thinking. "Okay, maybe I didn't. He had letters of recommendation from very prestigious firms."

188

"We have word that Willows was wanted in three states for embezzling from his companies. Now he may be hitting yours." Brege said.

"Morty, what were you and Willows arguing about at the convention center?" I asked.

Morty stopped to think again. "Oh, yeah. I wasn't happy with the reports Willows was giving me. He was stalling on turning them in. I was annoyed about it and told Willows. I mentioned to Willows that Dick Lawrence was snooping and told me he had something on Willows and was going to tell me about it. Dick said he still had things to find out. Oh, God, did I get Dick murdered?"

I looked to Brege, "Morty may be a crook, and dumb, but I don't think he'd be involved in murder. Willows found out through Morty that Lawrence was gathering info on his embezzlements and had him hit." I turned back to Morty. "Why were Max and I set up for a hit? Did you hear us talking in the back of the booth?"

"You talking about when you and Max were in the back of the booth?"

"Yes, didn't you hear us?"

"I was watching the girls sell, Willows came into the booth with me and he was back by the curtain. He would have heard you two talking, not me. He left just before you two came out."

"I'd say we need Willows," Brege said. "Shay, you need to stay with us for a day or two more. Your life could be in danger if Willows thinks you are talking to us."

I could see Morty turn pale, "You think he may want me dead?"

"It's possible, besides, I may need to talk to someone in the IRS about your activities." Brege said with a grin.

Morty turned three shades paler. Brege stood and I followed him out of the room. Brege told the cop at the door to take him back to his cell. We walked back towards his office.

"Not much we can do now until we find Willows. He could be way out of the city by now if he thinks we're on to him. I got his apartment being watched, and your publishing company. I have a feeling he's not coming back."

"Any way you can find out where he has his funds hidden?"

"I already have my tech people digging into his accounts, if they find them. Hell, he may have the money stuffed in a mattress somewhere. He's eluded officials in three states. He's no dummy like Morty is."

"With Morty in jail, I wonder who's going to be watching the booth?" I said, thinking about the bubble-headed girls and all that money from sales.

"Doesn't Morty have an assistant?"

"If he does, I don't know who it is. Well, since we are done here, I'll go to the convention center and see what's going on."

We got to the office, Max and Buck were gone. "Now where did they go off to?" Brege asked.

"They both aren't fond of police, so I guess they went out to the car. I'll talk later. If you find Willows, let me know. I have a speech to give tonight at the convention. You're welcome to come and listen. Bring your wife, Penny will be there."

"I may do that. I'll call if anything develops."

I said my good-byes and went out to the car. Max and Buck were standing with the goons, talking.

"Find out anything?" Buck asked.

"We don't think Morty was involved in the murders, but he's going to have to deal with the IRS now. Almost as bad as a murder charge. I need to go to the convention center."

Max signaled to the goons and everyone got in the car. Max drove to the center and dropped us off. Buck and the goons followed me into the center. I figured Max would find us. He probably hid a tracker on me when I wasn't looking.

I led my crew to the booth and found Shelly by herself. "Where's your partner?"

"Mr. Willows came by and said he needed her to help him with a project." Shelly replied.

I suddenly felt a chill. I pulled my cell phone and called Brege. "Lou, Willows was at the center and took one of the sales girls away."

"Think he's going to use her to make his escape?" Brege asked on the phone.

"I don't know. The girl here just said Willows wanted her to help him with something. I'll keep my eyes open here and let you know. But I'd say get some detectives down here in case."

"I got Willows picture off his warrant to give to my men, so I'm on it," he said and hung up. Max and Buck were together now and standing with the goons.

"Willows was here and took one of the girls from the booth, I don't know what he's up to, maybe using the girl to cover his actions."

"I saw what Willows looked like yesterday, I'll take my men and see if I can spot him," Max said.

"Good, I'll take Buck and follow up. Call me if you find him. Brege is sending some of his men, so we'll have back up."

I took Buck and went back to Shelly. "Did Willows say what he wanted?"

"No, just he needed Jamie to help him."

"Which way did they go?"

She looked around then said, "I wasn't happy to be left here alone, so I watched them go. Willows took her through that door over there." She point to a door on the side of the room. I took Buck and we ran for the door. It was unlocked and we went in. It was a hallway going along the outside of the arena. It only went one way, so we followed it.

We came to what must be the employees area, kitchen and janitorial. There were a number of staff running about. I saw one man standing at a podium. I figured he must be a supervisor. I went to him and asked if he saw a man and a young girl go through here.

"Yeah, about an hour ago. The guy looked too old for the girl, so I asked what he was doing. He said he was looking for the conference rooms. I told him he wasn't anywhere near them and to get out."

"Where did they go?"

"Through that door, to the outside parking lot."

I thanked him and we went outside. I looked around but there were hundreds of cars and people walking about. My cell phone rang and the caller ID said it was Brege. I answered.

"Jim, Willows was spotted at the publishing house. He had the girl with him."

"As soon as I find Max we'll be there." I hung up and called Max and told him what was going on. I said we'd meet at the front of the building. Buck and I ran around the outer side of the building until we got to the front doors.

Max and the town car came screeching up and stopped fast. Max yelled to get in.

*

Chapter 26

I knew the address of the publishing house, but not where it was. Max said he knew, so we got there in quick time. We pulled up to the front of the building and I saw Brege standing with a couple people. I got out of the car, followed by Buck and the goons, and went to Brege.

"What's the status?" I asked.

"Willows is inside holding the girl hostage." Brege said. "He must have some business inside to risk coming here."

"Maybe he has to access the computers to get to his money."

"Or destroy all the evidence that he was involved in embezzling the funds," Brege added. "We're ready to go in."

We went to the front doors of the building and in. It was Sunday, so the place should be empty, but Willows left the doors unlocked. Strange, I thought. Max and Buck were behind me, followed by Gino's men.

Big Apple Murders

We moved to the accounting offices as stated by the map at the door. We went down a long hall and then I saw more cops coming from the other end. They must have come in the back way. We heard movement coming from one room, and then a girl screamed. Brege and two of his men ran to the open door and were going to enter when the gun fire started.

Everyone dropped to the ground. Brege's men, who were in the SWAT gear, came to the door and entered, being careful not to shoot the girl. They found the room empty except for the girl. One officer yelled clear and Brege rushed in.

He approached the girl and asked, "Where did he go?"

She looked panicky as Brege cut her bonds on her wrists. "He went out that door," she said, nodding to the door. Brege pointed to his men and they streamed out.

The girl sat on a chair Brege pulled over for her. "What was he doing in here?"

"I don't know. He was doing something on the computer. He didn't say anything."

I went to the computer and saw it was opened to an accounting program. The columns had no money listed and the total was just as blank. "It looks like he cleaned out the entire company funds. It's showing no balance. Great, there goes my royalties."

"He had to do it here, which is why he came here. Bringing the girl was his safety net. I wonder why he didn't take her?" Brege said.

"He could move faster without dragging her along," Max said behind me.

"Very true, Max. Well, we're back to chasing him. Jim, do you know where he transferred the funds to?" Brege said.

I was still by the computer. "Nope, he may have closed the transfer point before he closed the company files. Maybe your people can get into it."

He pulled his cell phone and I heard him call for a CSI unit. We could hear gun fire again, coming from outside the building. Then it stopped.

We all headed to where we thought the shooting came from and found the SWAT men standing by the back parking lot. One officer came up and said, "He got away in a blue Mercedes, got the license and I called for a BOLO."

"He got his money, now he's on the run." I said.

I looked over and saw Max on his phone. I wondered who he was calling.

"Again, there's nothing we can do until we catch Willows." Brege said. "I'll have forensics dig into the computer and see where he moved the funds. Maybe we can catch them, or at least stop them."

Brege's cell phone buzzed and he answered. He smiled and said, "Yes, dear." I didn't figure it was the police calling. He listened and then hung up. "Seems my wife and yours are worn out from shopping. I didn't know they were going to do that."

"Believe me, it was my wife who started that. I know her. Well, it's up to your people to track down Willows, I have a speech to give, and a wife to see."

I turned to Buck and said, "We need to get back to the convention center. This is police business now."

Max dropped Buck and me off, and one of the goons hung around with us. I didn't object. Brege had Penny dropped at the center also, and we met at the food court.

"So, did you have a good time?" I asked her.

"Delightful. We had a splendid time," she replied. "Did you catch your killers?"

"Long story, I'll tell you later. Now, I want to enjoy my last day here at the convention before I have to speak."

"You need to put on your expensive new suit you bought for the occasion," she said.

"I know," I said, looking at my watch. It was just after four and I was supposed to talk around seven. "We need to go back to the hotel to get ready."

I called Max and said that we were walking back to the hotel. He tried to talk me into driving us. "Max, it's only just down the block. Besides, Louis is still with us and you know how well Penny shoots, so I'm safe."

He agreed and I asked him to come to my speech, he said he would. I hung up and we left the center.

"I should have tried on this suit before I bought it. The thing is a little big." I said as I looked at myself in the room mirror.

"More room to hide your guns and other weapons," Penny giggled.

"Not funny. I look like a kid at his confirmation. Last time I buy at the big and tall men's store."

"Suck it up, we need to get back to the center." She was pushing me to the door. I opened it and was surprised to see Max.

"You're going to your speech in the fancy car. No argument." Max said.

I didn't argue. We got Buck from his room and went to the car. Max drove us to the center and pulled up in front. He got out and came around to open the door. Classy.

Mrs. Nixon was at the entrance to the auditorium where I was to speak. She greeted us and took us back stage to a dressing room. My cell phone buzzed and it was Brege.

"I'm about to go on stage. Are you and the wife coming?"

"We're already here and seated in the audience, you got quite a crowd. I didn't think you were that popular," he said, with a chuckle.

"Did you call me to say you were here?"

"Nope, good news. Forensics got into the computer and Willows hadn't closed out the program properly. They managed to withdraw all the funds back to your publisher. They put a new password on it so Willows can't get back in."

"So, Willows is broke and on the run again," I said.

"Yep, and he's not going to be happy."

"Now that worries me. I usually get a visit by the bad guy who's mad because he blames me for messing up his crime. That's when Penny shoots him. I'll have to warn her to be ready."

"I can have some men on you in a blink."

"No, I got Max, Buck, and one of Gino's men. Then there's Penny. So I'm good."

"Okay, have a good speech," he said and hung up.

I told Penny and Buck what he said.

"I'll be ready," Penny said. I kissed her and we left the dressing room. Penny and Buck went through a door to the auditorium to find seats. Louis said he had to stick with me, I let him.

Mrs. Nixon came down the hall and said I could go to the stage anytime. Everyone was ready. She skittered off and I went to a door with a sign that said stage. We went through and the back of the stage was empty. I thought that was strange. Where were the union crew who managed the curtains and lights.

Louis said he was going to post himself on the side of the stage and went there. I was standing behind the curtain when I felt something at the back of my neck. I whispered, "Crap."

"I can't get to my money, so I'm going to take you hostage until they give it back. You seem to be someone they admire, so you got elected."

*

Chapter 27

"If I refuse to go with you, you'll lose your leverage. If you kill me, you'll lose your leverage. Either way, I'm not going with you." I said, trying to sound brave.

"Don't go all political on me. I can shoot your arm and you'll give in. Better yet, I can shoot your wife. How's that sound?"

"How about a third option. I shoot your head and watch it explode," came a voice from behind us.

I carefully turned my head and saw Max with two large men behind him. Max had his Magnum aimed at Willows' head. I could also see Willows weighing his options. I didn't want to die, so I hoped he picked the best option. Surrender.

I heard a struggle as Gino's men grabbed on to Willows and pulled his gun away. I moved away from them and watched as the two giants carried Willows out of the stage area. One had his hand over Willows mouth. Max came to me.

"I told you I know everything that goes on around you. Now, go make a good speech." Max said smoothly.

"What are you going to do with him?" I asked figuring he was going swimming.

"Don't you fret about that. We'll take good care of Mr. Willows." Max gave me a big smile and walked off.

Now I was worried for Willows. I heard Mrs. Nixon announcing my name and so I figured I'd go through the curtain to my doom.

The speech went well, if I do say so myself. I even told the story about an embezzling accountant who was just taken away by the mob. I had spotted Brege in the third row and could see he caught my reference. I knew he'd want a piece of Willows when the mob finished with him. Penny and Buck were in the front row and I introduced her, having her come up to the stage. She had Willy with her. Poor dog missed out on all the earlier excitement. She came up with a big smile and I told everyone of her expertise with a gun. I took questions, but they were mostly aimed at Penny. I let her have her moment.

It was all over and everyone was gathering at the stage. Brege whispered that Max had turned over Willows to the police. I said I had hoped he would swim with the fishes. Brege laughed.

We all ended up at a very nice restaurant that Brege recommended. Food was good and the ambiance was great. I saw a few things that I would recommend to Angelo.

We finished there and Brege and his wife went off. Max drove us to the hotel and we thanked him.

"What time is your flight in the morning?" Max asked. I told him. "I'll come by to take you there. See you in the morning." He drove off.

"I think we have a new friend," I said.

"Just don't invite him to stay in our guesthouse," Penny said.

I grinned.

"You already invited him out to Vegas, didn't you?"

"I just said if he wanted to go on a vacation, we had a place he could stay in."

"I hope he knows how to make breakfast," Penny smiled and went into the hotel.

The next morning, we had our bags packed and Max picked us up. He delivered us to the airport and drove us to our charter plane. I was surprised to see Brege and Harris there.

"Come to make sure we leave the city?" I said, as I exited the car.

"Had to fill you in on Willows. He's in custody, thanks to the family." He nodded to Max. "We have a lot on him, so it's going to be a slam dunk for prosecution. Good news, too. Willows did know the Hangman, they're related. Willows wanted it known he didn't commit the murders so, he's fingering the Hangman for hiring him to do the two authors. The first author was a mistake, poor guy. We're tracking down the Hangman now. Won't be long and we'll have a serial killer off the streets. So, have a nice flight. Come back again, but not too soon."

Everyone helped put our bags in the plane and we boarded. I waved to our friends as the plane taxied out.

Big Apple Murders

Five hours later we landed in Vegas at McCarron Airport. We had left the new company van at the hangers and loaded everything on. I drove to our house. Buck got his bags and put them in his car and drove off.

I took Willy for a run around the yard. He was happy to be home. We threw our bags in the living room and got in the Crown Vic. I drove us to the office and we went in. Lacey looked up and smiled.

"I hope you two had a nice time in New York," she said.

"Are you the Lacey we left here?" I asked.

"Yes, I'm relaxed since I didn't have to put up with you for a few days. How was your stay?"

I looked at Penny and said, "Wouldn't you say it was a little boring?"

"I would, nothing great about the Big Apple is there?"

We smiled and went to my office. I heard Lacey say, "Weirdos."

Penny steered me to the new break room. We stopped at the door and Penny said, "I had Lynn set this up for me. Hope you enjoy it."

She opened the door and all our friends were in the room yelling surprise. I jumped and nearly knocked over Lacey behind me. The room was decorated with streamers and balloons, and there was a cake on a table. We went in and Penny said, "It's the anniversary of the day you got your P.I. license. That started this all. It's been a great ride. Thank you, sweetie."

THE END

For every ending, there's a new beginning.

Here's a preview of the next book, "Kennel Murders"

Chapter 1

It was a yap fest in the dark room as the two men walked among the cages of excited dogs. They had flashlights and were examining the cards on the cages, looking for certain canines. The fancier the breed, the better. After a half hour, they had what they wanted and took the large box out to their van. They slid the box into the back and drove off. In the morning, the kennel employees would realize they had been robbed.

~~*~~

When a person gets to a certain age, they shouldn't be doing anything dangerous to their health. Okay, in all fairness, I was in a dangerous business. My private investigating firm had its share of dangerous cases, especially when it came to murder. I have this curse, murder seems to follows me. Or, so my wife keeps telling me. But I'm getting away from the point. I get involved in dangerous activities, and this was one of them.

No, not murder or any such thing that would glorify my situation. Here's what happened; I brought out the ladder from the garage and proceeded to try and change the spotlight on the corner of the house, the one that lights the driveway at night. I really should have had someone hold the ladder for me, but I'm a careful person. Or so I thought.

I was only about five feet off the ground when I turned the wrong way and my foot missed the step. I came down on my left leg and just knew something was wrong when I felt, and heard, the cracking sound from my lower leg. I also knew when I couldn't stand that something was terribly wrong.

Penny, my wife and famous talk show host, was out by the pool. The noise from our ugly Greek statue pouring water into the koi pond was just loud enough to cover my cries for help. I pulled my cell phone out and dialed her. Luckily, she had her phone by the pool with her.

"Hello? Are you getting too lazy to come talk to me in person?" she said before I had a chance to talk. She did that a lot.

"Okay, dispense with the pleasantries, I need help out front. It seems I broke my leg and I could use you out here now." I replied.

"Are you in pain?"

"Well, if you broke your leg, wouldn't you be in pain?"

"Okay, I'll be right there. Should I call an ambulance?"

"I'm not sure yet. Just come see if you can help me up and I'll decide."

I heard her hang up and I waited. Shortly, she came around the side of the house and over to me on my back, flat out on the ground.

"Sweetie, are you all right?" she asked.

"I doubt it seriously. Help me to stand and I'll see if I need an EMS unit."

She helped me to sit, then tried to bring me up to my feet. As soon as I put weight on my left leg, I went down again. The pain was worse than when I fell the first time. I hated pain, so I gasped for her to call for help.

She dialed 911, and then called my office to see if Buck was in. He was, so she told him what happened and he said he'd be right out.

I'm sure Buck broke a lot of traffic laws, but he arrived before the ambulance.

Bob Moats

"Damn, Jim, you should know better than to climb a ladder without someone to help," he said, half grinning. "You could have called me."

"I didn't want to disturb anyone. My vacation is getting boring and all I've done is odd jobs around the house."

We heard the EMS unit roaring up the street, sirens blaring. I was pretty much known by the medical teams as they have been to my house numerous times to patch up criminals. They pulled into the drive and came over to me.

"Mr. Richards, you aren't supposed to be the one hurt." One med tech said.

"It was a dangerous criminal who attacked me then ran off."

They looked at the ladder still standing and grinned.

"Got to watch out for those dangerous criminal ladders," the other tech said as they studied my leg.

I winced in pain as they probed and pulled. "Yep, it looks broken," one man said and they brought out the inflatable splint and put it around my leg. Then they brought out the gurney and carefully put me on it.

I looked at Penny and said, "If I don't make it, give everything I own to charity."

She smiled and said, "Like hell, I'll sell it all and go on a cruise."

"You are so caring," I said, as they put me in the van.

Buck yelled, "I'll bring Penny to the hospital after she changes. Anyone you want me to call?"

"Yeah, my lawyer. I'm going to sue the ladder." The tech closed the door.

I was looking at the ceiling of the EMS unit and wondering how long I was going to be out of commission. We arrived at the hospital and they wheeled me into the ER. I spent the next two hours being poked, probed, and x-rayed enough to tell me what I already knew. I had a broken leg.

I found Penny and Buck waiting in the private room I requested after the nurse brought me back from having my leg plastered. They set the leg back in place and said I'd probably be on the cast for a while. They weren't being time specific, seeing as I was an "older" person, my bones may not heal as fast. But they said I'd be up and around on crutches.

"Damn, this messes up my vacation," I said to Penny.

"Jim, the whole point of you taking time off was to do some work around the house. Which you've neglected since we moved in. Now you have an excuse to not do anymore work."

"I can hire someone to do all that stuff," I said.

"Should have thought of that before you climbed the ladder," Buck said from his chair by the bed.

"Thanks for the afterthought. How's the office doing?"

"Earl and Trapper are busy on domestic cases and Lynn is off tracking down a missing person who came to Vegas to gamble. Probably lost his shirt and is hiding downtown in bar. I've got nothing right now, so I can help you get around."

"Thanks Buck. I appreciate it. The doctor said I could leave tomorrow after they get me up and walking with crutches."

"I'll have to go to work at the studio, so you'll have to fend on your own around the house," Penny said.

Buck said, "I'll come over to baby sit him in the morning."

"Will you make my toast and take me out for a walk?" I asked him.

"Do you want me to bathe you, too?" he said with his famous walrus grin.

"I don't think that will be necessary. A sponge bath would be nice though. Penny, you could dress like a nurse and sponge bathe me."

"Ha! Buck can dress like a nurse and take care of it." Penny said.

"I'm not shaving my legs to dress like a nurse. No sponge baths from me. You can do that for yourself," he said with a smirk now.

Penny kissed my forehead and said she had to go in early tomorrow to her studio. "We're having a show about the big dog competition this week at the MGM Grand arena. The studio will have lots of dogs and I want to get settled with them. I'll take Willy with me, to show him off."

"He'd win all the prizes, I'm sure. Lot of fancy breeds in the show?"

"Yep, all future winners in their categories," Penny said.

"Reminds me of the time I had to act as bodyguard for that dog in the dog show back in Michigan." Buck said.

"I'm sure it will be the same thing. But no killer sons to worry about," Penny said as she got ready to leave with Buck. "See you tomorrow, sweetie." She kissed me again and they left.

I turned on the TV that I ordered for the room, put the bed up in a sitting position, and thought, this wasn't too bad.

**

Continued in the book…

~~*~~

Big Apple Murders

Jim Richards Family of Readers

Thanks to the following people who are now part of the Jim Richards Family of Readers. They have read a book or more and enjoyed them. They all volunteered to be included in the list. If you are a fan of the books, send me your full name and you will be included in future books. Send your name to murdernovels@bobmoats.com to be added here and on the website. (updated 3-30-14)

* Achim Feifel * Al Norris * Alex Wheatley * Alexandra Delporte-Wilkinson * Amy Tapia * Andrea Bryan * Anne Shepherd * Arianda Sugar * Arlene Markowski * Ashley Augustus * Audra Hall * Barbara Hughes * Barbara Sammons * Barbara Schuler * Barbara Zirger * Beth Donohue Plenskofski * Betsy Childress * Beth Gibson * Bill Sandy * Bill Tornquist * Billie-jo Collie * Boni J Rychener * Carl Bishopric * Carla Lewis * Carole Henderson * Carolyn Conroy * Carolyn Riddle-Linington * Cassy Bailey * Chad Hudson * Charlotte L Duran * Cheryl L. Everett * Cindy Ackley Nunn * Cindy Valstad * Connie Bancroft * Corinne Kay O'Daniel * Dana Robbins Chuchran * Dana Wichita * Danielle Monique * Darren Heald * Dave Travers * David Wilkinson * DeAnn Jannereth * Deanna Miller * Deb Breuker Balbo * Debbie Carter * Debbie White * Deborah Fartuch * Deborah Gauze * Deborah Sullivan * Dee King * Denise Freeman * Diana Carver * Dixie Beck * Donna Gould * Donna Thompson * Donny Minter * Doris Kight * Eddie Moore

Bob Moats

* Eric Walters * Felicia Annette Bradfield * Francine Menor * Gail Chesney * Georgiann Minster * George Conner * Greg Colucci * Hayley Rankin * Harold Garcia * Heidi Arnold * Irma Ranee Coy * Jacqueline Moss * Jan Kimball * Janice Schneider * Janice Spoor * Jennifer Redmond * Jessica Keown-Belous * Jim Beck * Jo Boguslaw * Jo Turner * Joanne Marie Turner * John Peiffer * John Wisbiski * Joseph Wauro * Joyce Stacy * Joyce Trifiletti * Judy Franklin * Judy Travers * Judy Padgett * Julie Heath * Junnahvee Benson * Karen Dahl * Karen Grams * Karen Higham * Karen Kaiser * Karen Meinburg Richwine * Karen Kirkman Parker * Karin Hawkins * Karin Vasvari * Kathleen Donohue Roesing * Kathleen Riddle-Wolfe * Kathy Hinds Moore * Kathy Jones * Kathy Mitchell * Katie Benzler * Kay Burns * Kelly Garcia * Ken Boggs * Keota Rodriguez * Kiera Mccarthy * Kim Estes * Kitty Stolle * Kristie Sciler * Kirsty Stanton * LaLonnie Scallen * Larry Morris * Leann Parr * Lenora Scales * Leslie Marie Jackson * Linda Forester * Linda Ingle Cox * Linda Kennerö * Linda Magill * Lisa Bower * Liz Gibson * Lorraine Wiman * Loretta Alexander * Lynda Bowles * Lynette Lawrance * LuAnn Louttit * Manny Rothman * Marcia Gibson DeWitt * Marie Calder * Marlene Bryan * MaryLouise Kramp * Mary Lynn Gross * Megan Atkins * Meghan Hyden * Melody Cannavan * Michael Carruthers * Michael Dinkens * Michael Vannoy * Michelle Burns-Mitchell * Michelle Pilcher * Micki Potter * Mike Moats * Mimi Baur * Myrna Hecht * Nadine Sutton * Natalie Quine * Neena Martin * O'Della Wilson * Pat Pollington * Pat Rohn * Patricia Jarmon * Patricia C Trezza * Patrick Barry * Paul Lawrance * Peggy Davis * Phyllis Bassett * Raylene Matheny * Rebecca Collins Besner * Renee Brumley * Reta Hanna * Reta Moats * Roberta Navarro-Harder * Sally Berneathy * Sally Hubler * Sarah Santos *

Big Apple Murders

Satka Nikc * Sharon E. Edwards * Sharon Mangini * Sharon McMillon * Sheena Rawl * Sherry Amstutz * Shirley Alvarez * Shirley Davies * Shirley Williams * Stacie Rowe * Stephanie Conner * Steve Cullen * Susan Haughton * Susan Hesse Adams * Susan Salomon * Suzan K Chase * Taisha Cullum * Tamara Moore * Tammy Castleberry * Tammy Lynn Wood * Ted Murphy * Terri Atkins * Terri Creech * Terry Raab * Tonia Rachael Riggs-Williams * Travis Fleury-Lopez * Twyla Gawlas * Val Brooks * Walt Munsel * Yvonne Isakson *

Thank you to all these wonderful people.

Thank you for purchasing this book. I hope you enjoy it as much as I enjoyed writing it for my faithful readers. Please feel free to email me to tell me what you thought about my stories. I love hearing from readers. I can be reached at murdernovels@bobmoats.com thanks again!

*